P9-CKR-936

The Communication Cord

by the same author

CRYSTAL AND FOX
PHILADELPHIA, HERE I COME!
THE FREEDOM OF THE CITY
LIVING QUARTERS
VOLUNTEERS
FAITH HEALER
TRANSLATIONS

The Communication Cord

BRIAN FRIEL

ff

FABER AND FABER
London & Boston

First published in *1983*
by Faber and Faber Limited
3 Queen Square London WC1N 3AU
Printed in Great Britain by
Latimer Trend & Company Ltd Plymouth
All rights reserved

© *Brian Friel, 1983*

All rights in this play are reserved to the Proprietor.
All applications for professional and amateur rights
should be addressed to Spokesmen, 1 Craven Hill,
London W2 3EP

CONDITIONS OF SALE

*This book is sold subject to the condition that it shall not, by way
of trade or otherwise, be lent, resold, hired out or otherwise
circulated without the publisher's prior consent in any form of
binding or cover other than that in which it is published and
without a similar condition including this condition being
imposed on the subsequent purchaser*

Library of Congress Cataloging in Publication Data
has been applied for

British Library Cataloguing in Publication Data

Friel, Brian
The communication cord.
I. Title
822'.914   PR6056.R5
ISBN 0-571-13092-5

For
TOM PAULIN

CHARACTERS

TIM GALLAGHER
JACK MCNEILIS
NORA DAN
CLAIRE HARKIN
SENATOR DOCTOR DONOVAN
SUSAN DONOVAN
BARNEY THE BANKS
EVETTE GIROUX

Place
A restored thatched cottage close to the sea in the
remote townland of Ballybeg, County Donegal.

Time
The present, early in October; a sunny, gusty afternoon (Act 1) and that evening (Act 2).

The Communication Cord was first presented by Field Day Theatre Company at the Guildhall, Derry, on 21 September 1982. The cast was as follows:

TIM GALLAGHER	Stephen Rea
JACK MCNEILIS	Gerard McSorley
NORA DAN	Pat Leavy
CLAIRE HARKIN	Fedelma Cullen
SENATOR DOCTOR DONOVAN	Kevin Flood
SUSAN DONOVAN	Ann Hasson
BARNEY THE BANKS	Ian McElhinney
EVETTE GIROUX	Ruth Hegarty

Lighting by Rory Dempster
Designed by Margo Harkin
Music by Keith Donald
Directed by Joe Dowling

ACT ONE

The action takes place in a 'traditional' Irish cottage. The open-hearth fireplace, with the crook and the black hanging pot, occupies most of the wall right. (Left and right from the point of view of the audience.) A string is stretched across the breast of the fireplace as a clothes-line. Hanging on it is a pink night-dress. Downstage on the same wall is a door leading to a bedroom. The back wall contains most of the furnishings. Stage right, in the corner close to the fireplace, is a settle bed which is concealed behind curtains. Next to the bed is a kitchen table positioned in front of a small square window. The window is curtained with lace. Beside the table is a dresser, fully stocked with plates, cups, bowls, etc. Next to the dresser is the double door. When the big door is open we can see the half-door beyond it. Left of the door is a large churn; a creel for holding turf; a wooden flail. On the wall left there are three wooden posts complete with chains where cows were chained during milking. (A hundred years ago this was the area of the house where animals were bedded at night.)

A wooden stairway, beginning downstage left, leads up to the loft. This loft (unseen) is immediately above the kitchen. A substantial beam of wood at right angles to the kitchen floor supports the floor of this loft. This beam should be placed wherever it causes least masking—perhaps downstage right (below the fireplace) or downstage left (below the stairs).

Apart from a few chairs and stools (all 'traditional') the entire centre of the stage is free of furnishings.

Every detail of the kitchen and its furnishings is accurate of its time (from 1900 to 1930). But one quickly senses something false about the place. It is too pat, too 'authentic'. It is in fact a restored house, a reproduction, an artefact of today making obeisance to a home of yesterday.

TIM GALLAGHER *is in his late twenties/early thirties, a junior lecturer without tenure in a university. A serious, studious young man with a pale face and large glasses. The business of coping with everyday life makes him nervous and seems to demand more than ordinary concentration. He is relaxed and assured only when he is talking about his work: he is doing his Ph.D. in an aspect of linguistics. The enterprise he is now reluctantly embarked on has made him very agitated.*

JACK MCNEILIS, *his friend, is the same age. He is a barrister.* JACK *has all the characteristics that* TIM *lacks. He is quick-talking, self-confident, able to handle everybody and every situation. He considers himself to be a man of vast and worthwhile experience.*

We hear a motorbike approach the house. It stops. Voices off. Then the latch is lifted and the big door is pushed open. TIM *looks into the room across the half-door.*

TIM: It was open, Jack.

JACK: What?

TIM: The door—it wasn't locked.

(*Cut the sound of the engine.*)

JACK: Can't hear you.

TIM: The door was open.

JACK: You're turning the key the wrong way.

(TIM *looks at the key in his hand.*)

TIM: Am I?

JACK: Turn it clockwise—OK?

TIM: Yes.

JACK: Now just lift the latch and give it a good push.

TIM: Yes.

JACK: Got it now?

TIM: Yes.

JACK: Good.

(TIM *draws the bolt on the half-door and enters. He takes off his crash helmet, searches his pockets, finds a handkerchief and wipes his watering eyes. He searches his pockets again, finds his glasses, blows on them, cleans them and puts them on. Now he can see properly. He surveys the kitchen. He is wearing a dark, well-worn, three-piece suit, black shoes, white shirt and dark tie. He shudders occasionally from cold after the*

12

motorbike trip.

JACK *enters. He is carrying his helmet, an overnight bag and a*
plastic bag full of groceries. He is casually but carefully
dressed: a suede jacket, open-neck lemon shirt, tan trousers,
stylish shoes. Unlike TIM's *his appearance bears no signs of the*
journey and the ravages of the wind.

TIM *wanders around uneasily, looking vaguely and without*
much interest at the furnishings, touching them abstractedly.
JACK *closes both doors behind him as he enters and immediately*
begins unpacking—putting groceries on the dresser, his bag in
the bedroom, etc.)

(*Entering*) Two and a half hours exactly from the city
centre to the bottom of the lane there. That's not bad
going. And now you know why I haven't a Ferrari: at least
with the old Honda I can drive up that bloody lane, right up
to the door.

TIM: (*Scarcely hearing*) Yes.

JACK: When the parents or the sisters come for a weekend they
have to leave the car down at the main road and walk up.
It's hell in winter—water, muck, slush, bloody cow-
manure. You arrive soaked and spent. But father believes
that the penance of that introduction is somehow part of the
soul and authenticity of the place.

(*The big door blows open.* JACK *closes it.*)

That south wind hits the front of the house. Are you cold?

TIM: Just a bit.

JACK: I'll light the fire.

TIM: No, no. I'll be fine in a minute. Do you use it much?

JACK: Depends. When my services as the country's leading
barrister aren't in demand—which is nearly always; and as
often as I can ensure the company and the consolations of a
female companion. Make yourself at home.

TIM: Thanks.

JACK: Did you get a glimpse of the beach? It's just at the
bottom of that field.

TIM: Yes.

JACK: Dramatic, isn't it?

TIM: Yes.

13

(JACK *goes into the bedroom.*)

JACK: You might have time for a swim. But you'd need to be careful near the rocks at the far side—there's a heavy undertow.

(*In his abstracted way* TIM *is touching the pink night-dress on the line. He is vaguely aware of its incongruity here.*)

That's where Claire Harkin was nearly drowned—just below the sandbanks.

TIM: (*Alarmed*) When? Recently?

(JACK *enters. Almost guiltily* TIM *takes his hand quickly off the night-dress.*)

JACK: No; years ago. Here for Easter with the sisters and was almost dragged away. Artificial respiration; all that stuff. I'll take that (*crash helmet*).

TIM: You used to go with Claire, didn't you?

JACK: Lasted a week.

TIM: I always thought—

JACK: I'm exaggerating—two days. A golden rule, professor: never take out a friend of your sisters; from the word go the moral standard is pitched too high. Absolutely.

(*He produces a bottle of whiskey from his grocery bag and surveys it.*)

Too early for a charge, is it? Yes. Later—if there's time. (*He takes the bottle off to the bedroom.*)

You took her out a few times yourself, didn't you?

TIM: Claire?

JACK: We all thought that was terminal at the time. What happened between you?

TIM: Between Claire and me?

JACK: That's who we're talking about, isn't it?

(TIM *in some embarrassment is abstractedly and gently punching the beam with his fist.*)

TIM: Yes . . . oh that was years ago . . . a student thing . . . she—she—she—there was nothing much to—

JACK: (*Entering*) Don't touch that! Christ, man, do you want to bring the bloody loft down on us!

TIM: Sorry.

JACK: It's OK, professor. But that beam's only a temporary job we stuck up one day when the ceiling began to sag.

TIM: Sorry.

JACK: No harm done. We're getting a proper job done on it this winter. (*Looking around*) Well, what do you think of it?

TIM: I think my grandmother was probably reared in a house like this.

JACK: Everybody's grandmother was reared in a house like this. Do you like it?

TIM: It—it—it's very . . .

JACK: What?

TIM: Nice.

JACK: 'Nice'! The ancestral seat of the McNeilis dynasty, restored and refurbished with love and dedication, absolutely authentic in every last detail, and all you can say is 'nice'. For one who professes the English language, your vocabulary is damned limp. Listen, professor. (*In parody*) This is where we all come from. This is our first cathedral. This shaped all our souls. This determined our first pieties. Yes. Have reverence for this place. (*Laughs heartily.*) Come on; since it's going to be your property for the next few hours, you'd better know something about it. Hold on —let's get the timetable right first. Absolutely. (*Looks at his watch.*) What time do you make it?

(TIM *looks at his watch.*)

TIM: I forgot to wind it.

JACK: Wind it now, Tim. It's three o'clock exactly. When are Susan and Daddy Senator passing through?

TIM: She wasn't sure. She just said sometime after lunch. I think she said maybe sometime in the early afternoon.

JACK: You'd be a great witness.

TIM: I remember now. What she said was that her father had to be in Sligo at six for this political dinner he's speaking at.

JACK: That means he'll have to leave here at four thirty at the latest. Fine. Let's say they arrive at three thirty. So you'll have from three thirty until four thirty—one full hour. That should be adequate. I'll disappear for that hour—go for a swim, maybe—and the moment I see them leave I'll return and drive you down to the bus. Great.

(JACK *begins working again*.)

TIM: But you're going to be here, aren't you? I mean to meet them?

JACK: Like hell I am.

TIM: Jack, the understanding was that both of us were to—

JACK: You have misunderstood the understanding, professor. What I said was that I'd be happy to see Susan, with whom I once had a little fling, as you know, and for whom I still have a huge affection despite the fact that she is a sly, devious and calculating little puss, if you don't mind my saying so. But I made it clear to you that I would not meet Senator Doctor Donovan who went for me like a savage one night just because I was ten minutes late for a date with little Susan. 'My only child—my innocent little daughter'— I got all that stuff. No, sir. Oh don't be disarmed by the suave tongue of Dr Bollocks.

TIM: So that when they arrive I'm to be here alone?!

JACK: Absolutely. And not trembling, I hope. So that's the schedule. This is your house until four thirty. If for any reason they haven't left by then, you've got to get rid of them. Right?

TIM: Yes. But—

JACK: And the moment they leave, I'll return, drive you into the town on Brother Honda, put you on the evening bus, pick up Evette and bring her here. Excellent. Couldn't be simpler.

TIM: Evette? Evette who?

(JACK *does not know her surname*.)

JACK: Evette—Evette—Evette the French girl—from the Consulate—she's been around for years. What do you mean, 'Evette who'? The same Evette we bumped into at the party last Saturday. I promised I'd show her some of Donegal over the weekend. Right. That's the timetable. Mess it up and we're all in trouble.

(*The big door blows open. He closes it.*)

Must be something wrong with that latch. Now—the tour. (*Very rapidly*) A bedroom there, known as the 'room down'; one double bed. Fireplace. Usual accoutrements. Tongs.

16

Crook. Pot—iron. Kettle—black. Hob. Recess for clay
pipes. Stool. Settle bed. Curtains for same. Table. Chairs—

TIM: Slower—slower, Jack, please.

JACK: Have I lost you somewhere, professor? Where did I lose
you?

TIM: The settle bed.

JACK: Ah. This is the settle bed. Right?

TIM: Yes.

JACK: Absolutely. (*Rapidly again*) Table. Lamp. Window.
Curtains—lace. Clock—stopped. Dresser. Again the usual
accoutrements. Cups. Bowls. Plates—functional. Plates—
ornamental. Egg cups. (*Lifts bottle.*) Paraffin? (*Sniffs.*)
Vodka. Good. Give Susan a charge—not that she needs it.

TIM: I need it. Is there a glass?

JACK: A glass! The gaff's blown already. Bowls, professor,
bowls! Never glasses! Have you no sense of the authentic?
You *are* going to mess it. Door. Half-door beyond—even
though you can't see it, I assure you it's there. Churn.
Flail. Creel. Stairs to—

TIM: What's that again?

JACK: That is a creel.

TIM: No, that thing there.

JACK: That is a flail for—(*in exasperation*)—for special orgies on
midsummer night—an old and honoured Donegal ritual.
Two single beds up there. One beam or upright to support
the loft—and you're perfectly safe up there as long as some
fool doesn't shift this thing. Posts and chains for tethering
cows at night—a relict from the days when your granny and
the animals shared the same roof. And that's about it.
What else do you need to know?

TIM: It's not going to work, Jack.

JACK: Professor, you're—

TIM: I want to call it all off. It seemed a good idea in the
comfort of my flat—

JACK: Comfort?

TIM: —but I can see now that it's stupid and dangerous. It was
very kind of you to offer me your house—

JACK: My father's house.

17

TIM: Thank you very much. But I want to scrap the whole thing. It's crazy. For God's sake, I'm not even sure that I *like* Susan!

JACK: Who mentioned liking her, professor? You're going with her—that's all. And it's a perfect match: you're ugly and penniless, she's pretty and rich.

TIM: That's not why I'm going with her as you know damned well. And please stop calling me professor. I'm a bloody junior lecturer in linguistics. Without tenure.

JACK: But your thesis is nearly finished, isn't it?

TIM: I don't know. Maybe.

JACK: What's it on again?

TIM: Talk.

JACK: What about?

TIM: That's what the thesis is about—talk, conversation, chat.

JACK: Ah.

TIM: Discourse Analysis with Particular Reference to Response Cries.

JACK: You're writing your thesis on what we're doing now?

TIM: It's fascinating, you know. Are you aware of what we're doing now?

JACK: We're chatting, aren't we?

TIM: (*Warming up*) Exactly. But look at the process involved. You wish to know what my thesis is about and I wish to tell you. Information has to be imparted. A message has to be sent from me to you and you have to receive that message. How do we achieve that communication?

JACK: You just tell me.

TIM: Exactly. Words. Language. An agreed code. I encode my message; I transmit it to you; you receive the message and decode it. If the message sent is clear and distinct, if the code is fully shared and subscribed to, if the message is comprehensively received, then there is a reasonable chance —one, that you will understand what I'm trying to tell you—and two, that we will have established the beginnings of a dialogue. All social behaviour, the entire social order, depends on our communicational structures, on words mutually agreed on and mutually understood. Without that

18

agreement, without that shared code, you have chaos.

JACK: Chaos. Absolutely. Why?

TIM: Because communication collapses. An extreme example: I speak only English; you speak only German; no common communicational structure. The result?—chaos. Or when I was opening that big door, you were broadcasting on one wavelength, I was receiving on another. No shared context in which the common code can function. But let's stick with the situation where there is a shared context and an agreed code, and even here we run into complications.

JACK: So soon?

TIM: The complication that perhaps we are both playing roles here, not only for one another but for ourselves. But let's stick to basics. You ask me what my thesis is about. You ask me that question every so often and I tell you every time. Information requested; information transmitted; information received. But by the very fact of asking me as often as you do, you do something more than look for information, something more than try to set up a basic discourse: you desire to share my experience.

JACK: I don't—do I?

TIM: And because of that desire our exchange is immediately lifted out of the realm of mere exchange of basic messages and aspires to something higher, something much more important—conversation.

JACK: God.

TIM: A response cry! And that's really the kernel of my thesis. A response cry blurted out as an involuntary reaction to what you've just heard. And what does it tell me? Does your 'God' say: I never knew that before? Does it say: This is fascinating—please continue. Does it say: Yes, I do desire to share your experience. Does it say: Tim, you're boring me. Or is your expletive really involuntary? Maybe —because we're both playing roles, if we're both playing roles—maybe your 'God' is a *pretence* at surprise, at interest, at boredom. And if it is a pretence, why is it a pretence? Do you see the net we're weaving about ourselves now?

JACK: I do, professor. Absolutely. One—we're wasting time. And two—our plan goes ahead.

TIM: Plan? What plan?

JACK: This is your house for an hour.

TIM: O my God!

JACK: A response cry that goes straight past my heart. Or maybe it's a prayer: Please, God, receive my message.

TIM: Jack, I'm not going through with it! I'm not! I'm not!

JACK: Right. Right. Calm down. We've been over all this before. Will you trust me in this? Just trust me, Timothy, will you?

TIM: When someone says that to you, you know you're being betrayed. I'm sorry, Jack. I didn't mean that. I'm sorry. It's just that there's something shabby, something damned perfidious about the whole thing.

JACK: Wasn't it Susan's idea?

TIM: Hers—mine—yours—I've forgotten now how it originated. I think it began almost as a joke, didn't it? And suddenly here we are!

JACK: But she sees nothing unprincipled in it.

TIM: That worries me, too. Look at what I'm doing: for two furtive hours on a sunny October afternoon I'm to pretend I'm the owner of a–a–a–a miniature museum just because Susan thinks that would impress her pompous father who fancies himself as an amateur antiquarian.

JACK: One furtive hour.

TIM: All right. All right. One hour then.

JACK: And Dr Bollocks also happens to be a senator who can help you secure your tenure.

TIM: If that's how I were to get it, I'd refuse it.

JACK: Of course. The worthy and penniless Timothy Gallagher —all nobility and no nous. Look at it from Susan's point of view. Just because she's crazy about you—

TIM: Ah come on, Jack!

JACK: —is it unnatural that she should want her poor widowed father who dotes on his only child—and why wouldn't he? —what father wouldn't dote on such an estimable offspring? —is it unnatural, I ask you, that she should want him to share with her her regard, her respect, her admiration, yes,

20

yes, even her love for you?—is that unnatural?

TIM: Jack, I'm not a jury.

JACK: So they drop in here on their way to their political dinner and have a quick look round and Daddy Senator suddenly realizes that there's more to you than the stooped, whingeing, trembling, penniless, myopic, part-time junior lecturer without tenure. 'Good heavens, the lad has a noble soul like myself. Good gracious, this is a kindred spirit. My blessing on you both.' And her wealth that I once lusted after is safe in your pocket—or as near as bedamned. And they head off to address the party faithful and everybody's happy—Susan, Dr Bollocks, yourself.

TIM: It's still—

JACK: Shabby, furtive, perfidious, unprincipled. Dear God, surround me with people of no morals—(*sudden delight*)— Giroux!—that's her name!—Evette Giroux! How could that have slipped my mind? I'm away to the well for a bucket of the purest of pure spring water.

(*He picks up a wooden bucket and is about to exit when he sees* NORA DAN *passing the window.*)

Goddamnit, Nora Dan! The quintessential noble peasant— obsessed with curiosity and greed and envy.

(NORA DAN *knocks*)

Come in, Nora! (*Softly*) Distant relative of the family. Convinced this house is legally hers.

(NORA DAN *enters. She is in her sixties and single. A country woman who likes to present herself as a peasant.*)

NORA: Ah, Jack.

JACK: How are you doing, Nora?

NORA: Ah sure I'm only half-middling, Jack. You're welcome— you're welcome. And who's this young gentleman?

JACK: Tim Gallagher, a friend of mine. Nora Dan.

NORA: A friend of yours. Isn't that grand? You're welcome, sir, welcome.

TIM: Thank you, Mrs Dan.

NORA: (*Laughs.*) 'Mrs Dan'! Glory be to God, isn't that a good one! Sure I was never a missus in my life, Tim. I get the Dan from my father—that's the queer way we have of

21

naming people about here. (*To* JACK) I didn't find yous coming. Are yous here long?

JACK: We've just arrived.

NORA: You have surely. And you'll be staying for the weekend?

JACK: I will, Nora. Tim's going home on the evening bus.

NORA: The evening bus. He must be a very busy man. And how's mammy and daddy and the girls?

JACK: They're fine, thanks. They send their love.

NORA: They do surely.

JACK: (*To* TIM) Nora very kindly looks after the house when we're not here. She's a far-out relation of mother.

NORA: Daddy.

JACK: Father. What is it?—a third cousin?

NORA: Second and third.

JACK: (*To* TIM) That's it.

NORA: Twice removed.

JACK: Twice removed.

NORA: I'm sure this gentleman has a powerful big job, too?

JACK: Tim works in the University.

NORA: In the University. Oh, he'll be the smart man.

JACK: Brilliant, Nora.

NORA: He is surely. And it'll be the big wages he'll earn in a place like that?

JACK: Absolutely. And what's the news about Ballybeg, Nora?

NORA: Ah sure what news would there be in a place like this? Sure we see nobody and hear nothing here. I'm sure you were never in as backward a place as this, Tim?

TIM: No—yes—oh, yes.

NORA: You were surely—you're a travelled man. (*To* JACK) And how's Miss Tiny? I often think of Miss Tiny.

JACK: (*Embarrassed*) Who's that, Nora?

NORA: Miss Tiny—the big lady that was here with you last month.

JACK: Oh, Tiny—Tiny—she's—a—she's fine—she's fine.

NORA: She's fine, thanks be to God. (*To* TIM) I'm sure you know Miss Tiny?

TIM: I don't think I ever—

NORA: Oh, a great big stirk of a girl. Black as your boot and a

22

head of wee tight curls on her like a lamb in March. She used to lie all day in the salt water, rolling about like a big seal—Lord, and not a stab on her! Patsy the Post—(*to* JACK) you know Patsy—wee Patsy was cycling home from Mass that Sunday morning and looked down and there she was, stretched out on her back in the water; and d'you know, didn't the poor man fall off his bike and into the tide! And you know yourself, Jack, there's no more modest man in Ballybeg than Patsy—married with nine children. He said afterwards that he thought it was a porpoise through the salmon nets. Lord, it was the talk of the town!

JACK: Did I notice a caravan at the far end of the sandbanks, Nora?

NORA: (*To* TIM) He misses nothing, the same Jack. (*To* JACK) Indeed and you did. He's a German gentleman. I couldn't tell you his right name; all he gets about here is Barney the Banks but sure that wouldn't be his real name at all, would it?

JACK: Unlikely.

NORA: Unlikely, indeed. He's about the same age and build as yourself. A civiler man you couldn't meet except when he has—(*indicates drinking*)—you know yourself; and he'd be apt to gulder a wee bit then. But no harm in him; no harm at all. And he has me deaved asking about this house—says he never seen anything like it and he'd give a fortune to buy it. (*To* TIM) You know the way strangers get queer notions about a place like this; and foreigners is the worst. (*To* JACK) I gave him daddy's address but I'm sure he never wrote, did he?

JACK: Not that I know of.

NORA: Not that you know of. Ah, sure what would a foreign gentleman want to be living in a backward place like this for anyway? Yous have plenty milk and potatoes?

JACK: We're fine, Nora, thanks.

NORA: Yous are fine surely. Well, yous'll want peace for your holidays. I've just made a wee cake of soda bread—I'll bring yous over some of it later. Enjoy yourself now, Tim.

TIM: Thank you.

NORA: Not that yous'll have much chance to spend your fortune about here. But sure the three of yous'll make your own fun together.

JACK: See you later, Nora.

(*She leaves.* TIM *laughs.*)

What's she talking about—'the three of yous'?

TIM: 'He misses nothing, the same Jack.'

JACK: That's because the moment I first saw her I recognized her as a nosey, hypocritical, treacherous old bitch. Now she'll be over every half-hour, smelling around. Maybe you should light the fire.

TIM: How do I light it?

JACK: How would he light it? As our forebears lit it for thousands of years—by rubbing flint stones together!

(*Again he picks up the bucket and exits.* TIM *goes to the fireplace and studies it.* JACK *suddenly reappears at the half-door.*)

What about this, professor? When Susan and Daddy Senator are here I'll appear disguised as Barney the Banks and offer you a fortune for the place.

TIM: For God's sake, Jack—

JACK: It's not a bad idea, you know. (*Loudly, in German accent*) 'I hear you sell your house, Herr Gallagher—ja? I give you a fortune to buy it.'

TIM: Jack!

JACK: Of course you'll scorn the notion of flogging your heritage—and in Dr Bollocks's eyes your stock will rise even higher. You'll have tenure before the night's out!

TIM: How is it you never told me about Miss Tiny?

JACK: 'A million Deutschmark, Herr Gallagher. I hoffer you any monies you hask for.'

TIM: Was she really as black as your boot?

JACK: (*With dignity*) You know, Tim, there are times when you surprise and disappoint me. Tiny was a princess from Mysore; and her skin was the colour of ripe damsons; and it so happens that when she went back to India a part of me died. Bastard!

(*He disappears.*

TIM *looks at his watch, shakes it, holds it against his ear. His anxiety returns. He goes to the dresser, picks up the vodka bottle, chooses a cup, decides against a cup, takes a bowl, pours himself a large drink and drinks some of it quickly. He now returns to the fireplace (and again notices the night-dress) and feels along the top of the mantelpiece where he finds a box of matches. He strikes a match and holds it—at arm's length and with his face averted as if the fire were dangerous—against a piece of turf he holds in his hand. The turf does not ignite. The match burns his fingers and dies. He picks up his bowl and drifts off to explore the bedroom.*

CLAIRE *enters. She is about 30—competent, open, humorous. She is bare-footed and dressed in jeans and a T-shirt. She is carrying a wet, bright yellow, two-piece swimsuit and is drying her hair as she enters. She leaves her towel across the back of a chair and hangs the wet swimsuit on the clothes-line. She takes matches from the mantelpiece and lights the fire. It ignites instantly. She takes her night-dress from the line and goes upstairs.*

TIM *reappears. Again he looks at his watch. He drinks again from his bowl. He looks at the fireplace and immediately notices that the night-dress has been replaced by the swimsuit. He fingers the swimsuit and discovers it is wet. His bewilderment increases. He looks around—there is nobody there. He fingers the swimsuit again, could it belong to . . . ?)*

TIM: (*Calling gently*) Nora Dan?
(*Silence. Now he sees that the fire is lit. He stoops down to have a closer look and is suddenly enveloped in a blow-down.*)
O my God!
(*He staggers, coughing, into the centre of the kitchen and—as he did on his first entrance—takes off his glasses, dries his eyes, cleans the glasses.*
CLAIRE *has heard the noise downstairs.*)
CLAIRE: (*Off*) Is that you, Nora?
(TIM *hears the voice which he thinks comes from the direction of the door.*)
TIM: I'm here, Jack.
CLAIRE: I'll be straight down.

TIM: Who's there?

(CLAIRE *appears at the top of the stairs. She is wearing a dress now and is brushing her hair.*)

CLAIRE: Who's that?

TIM: Just a minute. I'm—

CLAIRE: Who are you? What do you want?

(TIM *now has his glasses on. He looks up and recognizes her.*)

TIM: (*Undisguised joy*) O my God—it's Claire! O my God!

(*She comes down the remaining steps.*)

CLAIRE: Tim? Is it you?

TIM: Yes—yes! It's me—Tim! God, I'm glad to see you, Claire.

CLAIRE: I'm glad to see you, too.

TIM: And you were nearly drowned!

CLAIRE: Was I?

TIM: Yes!

CLAIRE: Just now?

TIM: No! Years ago! One Easter!

CLAIRE: Oh.

TIM: God, that was a close thing, Claire!

CLAIRE: It was. Yes.

(*Pause.*)

TIM: Must have been terrifying. There's a heavy undertow over there . . .

CLAIRE: What are you doing here, Tim?

TIM: I came with Jack.

CLAIRE: Jack McNeilis?

TIM: We've just arrived.

CLAIRE: For the whole weekend?

TIM: For an hour—three thirty to four thirty.

CLAIRE: That's all you can spare?

TIM: Jack says that should be adequate. Are you staying the weekend?

CLAIRE: Until next Wednesday.

TIM: God, I wish I could stay. I'm going home on the evening bus but Jack's staying on. Maybe I could sneak back for a few minutes after half four—I'll ask Jack if I can. You only just missed him. He's gone to the well wherever it is— you've been here before—I suppose you know where it is—

26

anyhow that's where he's away too, with a big wooden pail like Little Miss Moffat and pretending he's Barney the Banks, the German visitor that lives in the caravan, and guldering about 'hoffering me a million Deutschmark' if I would sell him this house—

(*As he tells this story he acts it: imitating Jack with his pail and Barney drinking and staggering and guldering, then suddenly, realization—and even greater panic than before.*)

O my God! Get out—get out—get out! Now! Now! They'll be here any minute!

(*He grabs her towel and thrusts it violently into her hands.*)

For God's sake, will you move! What else have you got? Have you stuff upstairs? Have you a case? O my God!

CLAIRE: (*With great concern*) Tim, are you not well? What's the—?

TIM: (*Shouts*) Will you for God's sake go!

(JACK *enters.*)

JACK: I'm off, professor. There's a big car stopped at the foot of the lane and two figures coming up the— (*He sees* CLAIRE.) Oh, Christ!

TIM: A response cry uttered to convey that the utterer finds the world disappointing.

JACK: What are you raving about?

CLAIRE: What are you two up to?

JACK: The question is: what are you doing here, Claire?

CLAIRE: I'm here at your mother's request—to keep an eye on your youngest sister, Elizabeth, who is arriving tomorrow morning—

JACK: Elizabeth?

TIM: You can't leave now, Jack—neither of you.

CLAIRE: And I'm here because I'm free until next Wednesday apart from one lecture on Tuesday morning which a friend is going to take for me.

TIM: We'll all stay. We'll all meet them. You two are married— you're on your honeymoon—I'm your best man—

CLAIRE: Is he drunk?

(TIM *runs to the door and peers furtively out.*)

JACK: Claire, many, many years ago you and I were fortunate

27

enough to experience and share an affection that is still one of my most sustaining memories. If that memory means anything to you—and I can't believe it doesn't—will you trust me now and please leave immediately?

CLAIRE: Trust you?! I never trusted you, Jack! What are you scheming at now?

JACK: I won't take offence at that, Claire. But if I give you my solemn word as an old friend and as a lawyer—

CLAIRE: Hah!

JACK: —that your presence here over this weekend—and Elizabeth's—may jeopardize Tim's entire academic future—

CLAIRE: In what way?

JACK: —and I am aware that you and he were much, much closer than you and I ever were—but if I give you my solemn word—

(TIM *has run back to them.*)

TIM: Susan's gone back to the car for something. He's at the bend in the lane.

CLAIRE: Susan? Who's Susan?

TIM: (*Totally wretched*) I can't go through with it alone, Jack. Both of you stay—please!

CLAIRE: (*Brightly*) Yes. The whole weekend.

JACK: You're a bloody bitch.

TIM: We'll all have a party!

JACK: (*To* TIM) And you're a bloody fool. (*He goes to the door.*) Remember—one hour. Then out—both of you!

(*He exits.* TIM *runs after him.*)

TIM: Jack—Jack—

CLAIRE: It's the sweet little Susan Donovan I've heard so much about!

TIM: It is not.

CLAIRE: So I've walked in on a love nest!

TIM: It's nothing of the kind, Claire.

DONOVAN: (*Off*) Hello. Hello. Anybody at home?

CLAIRE: I'm going to enjoy this.

TIM: I'm asking you, Claire—I'm begging you—

DONOVAN: (*Off*) Hello? Hello?

TIM: O my God!—your swimsuit—!

28

(*He runs to the fireplace and has just grabbed the top half of the swimsuit when he is enveloped in a blow-down. He responds as before—O my God!—coughing, eyes streaming. Glasses removed etc.* CLAIRE *watches him for a few seconds and then goes calmly and serenely upstairs.*

DONOVAN, *doctor and senator, enters as he knocks. He is about 60, well preserved, very conscious of his appearance. He exudes energy and confidence, and considers himself to be a man of great charm and persuasiveness as indeed he is, particularly with women, more particularly with young women.*)

DONOVAN: Anybody here? May I come in?

TIM: Hello. Yes. Of course come in—come in. I'm having some trouble with the fire. Hello. How are you, Doctor?

DONOVAN: I'm well, Tim. How are you?

(DONOVAN *asks this question with some deliberation because* TIM *is cleaning his glasses with a yellow bra.*)

TIM: Busy—busy. Just—you know—just doing a bit of dusting. (*He thrusts the wet bra into his pocket and holds out his hand.*) I was afraid you mightn't have been able to find the house. (*For the next five minutes* TIM's *first concern is to establish* CLAIRE's *whereabouts.*)

DONOVAN: It wasn't too difficult. One old man we asked for directions said there were no Gallaghers in Ballybeg. Insisted your name must be McNeilis!

(*Seeing* TIM *looking around*)

Susie'll be with us in a moment. She went back to the car for our things.

TIM: Things?

DONOVAN: Our cases.

TIM: Suitcases?!

DONOVAN: They're not heavy. She can manage. (*Looking around*) Yes—yes—yes—I'm very glad we made the detour—this is certainly worth seeing. How long have you got it?

TIM: For an hour—oh, you mean—? Oh, years, years. It belonged to a second and third cousin of daddy's—father's.

DONOVAN: Really?

TIM: Twice removed.

29

DONOVAN: Do you use it much?

TIM: Occasionally—frequently.

DONOVAN: The journey is a bit long but then you're free a lot. You're still only part time, aren't you?

TIM: Yes.

DONOVAN: So Susie told me. Too bad.

TIM: But I'm hoping to get tenure when I finish my thesis.

DONOVAN: (*Looking around, not listening*) Yes . . . yes . . .

TIM: It's on Discourse Analysis with Particular Reference to Response Cries.

DONOVAN: Good Lord.

TIM: Exactly. That sort of thing.

DONOVAN: What sort of thing?

TIM: 'Good Lord'.

DONOVAN: Good Lord what?

TIM: That response cry—the imprecation—the expletive. We think we say things like 'Good Lord' casually but of course we don't. Yes, it is a conventionalized utterance but what is distinctive and interesting about it are three things: its form —you didn't, for example, say 'Oh shit' even though in different circumstances you might; the occasion of its utterance—during a not-too-relaxed, slightly formal exchange between myself and yourself; and most particularly its social function—you used it not as a response to what I was saying but merely as a reassuring sound that would encourage me to continue talking.

DONOVAN: Did I?

TIM: Yes.

DONOVAN: Good L. Imagine that.

(*Pause.*)

TIM: It's nice, isn't it?

DONOVAN: What?

TIM: The place.

DONOVAN: Nice? It's magnificent, Tim. Really magnificent. This is what I need—this silence, this peace, the restorative power of that landscape.

TIM: Yes.

(*Another pause.* DONOVAN *is standing in the middle of the*

30

kitchen, poised, listening, absolutely still, only his eyes moving.)
It's very nice indeed.

DONOVAN: This speaks to me, Tim. This whispers to me. Does that make sense to you?

TIM: Yes.

DONOVAN: And despite the market-place, all the years of trafficking in politics and medicine, a small voice within me still knows the responses. I was born in a place like this. Did you know that? No, how could you. In County Down. A long, long time ago, Tim. Politics has its place—of course it has. And medicine, too, has its place—God knows it has. But this, Tim, this transcends all those . . . hucksterings. This is the touchstone. That landscape, that sea, this house —this is the apotheosis. Do you know what I'm saying?

TIM: Yes.

DONOVAN: I suppose all I'm really saying is that for me this is the absolute verity. Am I talking nonsense?

TIM: No.

DONOVAN: I envy you, Tim. You know that, don't you?

TIM: Yes.

DONOVAN: That's not true. I don't envy you. You know that, don't you?

TIM: Yes.

DONOVAN: I'm happy for you. I rejoice for you because I think you hear that small voice, too, and I think you know the responses. Thank God for this, Tim. (*He shakes himself as if he were freeing himself of a painful-pleasurable memory.*) Well! Aren't you going to show me around? What was it Susie told me?—that this was just four walls when you got it? I don't believe it! Is that true?

TIM: That's all. Only four.

DONOVAN: And you re-roofed it yourself?

TIM: Yes.

DONOVAN: And thatched it?

TIM: Yes.

DONOVAN: By yourself?

TIM: Yes.

DONOVAN: Good L—. Good man. What did you thatch it with?

31

TIM: Thatch.

DONOVAN: Straw or bent?

TIM: Straw.

DONOVAN: It's warmer than bent but not as enduring. Do you find that?

TIM: It's not as enduring but it's warmer.

DONOVAN: Right. What sort of scollops?

TIM: Oh, the usual.

DONOVAN: Hazel or sally?

TIM: Hazel.

DONOVAN: Not as resilient but they last longer. Is that your experience?

TIM: They last longer but they're not as resilient.

DONOVAN: Exactly. What's this the old Irish expression is? 'The windy day isn't the day to scollop your thatch.' Isn't that it? And this is your bedroom?

(TIM *catches his elbow to stop him going into the bedroom.*)

TIM: We'll look at this room first. That's just a bedroom in there.

DONOVAN: The 'room down'.

TIM: The 'room down'—that's it. One double bed. (*Then rapidly*) Fireplace. Usual accoutrements. Tongs. Crook. Pot—iron. Kettle—black. Hob. Recess for clay pipes. Stool. Settle bed. Curtains for same. Table. Chairs. Christ!

(*This expletive because he sees* CLAIRE *coming serenely down the stairs.*)

DONOVAN: (*Delighted*) And you've held on to the old posts and chains!

(TIM *signals frantically to* CLAIRE *to go back up. She sees his gestures but keeps coming down.* DONOVAN *is crouching down at the posts.*)

My God, Tim, that's wonderful, that's really wonderful! I haven't seen these for—my God, it must be over fifty years! And you've incorporated them into the kitchen as of course it should be because that is exactly as it was! Oh, you're no amateur at this, Tim! You know your heritage! Oh, you and I are going to have a lot to say to each other! Marvellous! Just marvellous!

(CLAIRE *is now at the bottom of the stairs and is approaching* them. *As she approaches,* TIM's *panic rises. He scarcely knows what he is saying.*)

TIM: This is where we all come from.

DONOVAN: Indeed.

TIM: This is our first cathedral.

DONOVAN: Amen to that.

TIM: This shaped all our souls. This determined our first pieties. This is a friend of mine.

(DONOVAN, *who has begun to look quizzically at* TIM—'*Surely the young man isn't mocking me?*'—*now turns.* CLAIRE, *silent and smiling, is right behind him. He gets quickly to his feet.*)

DONOVAN: Ah. Forgive me.

TIM: This is Dr Donovan. A doctor of medicine. He is also a senator. In the Senate.

DONOVAN: For my sins. How are you? Haven't we met somewhere before?

TIM: You couldn't have. She's from here.

DONOVAN: Ah.

TIM: She lives in a caravan at the far end of the banks. She's married to a German.

DONOVAN: Lucky German. When I was a younger man, I used to have some German—

TIM: She doesn't speak German. She's French. Her name is Evette.

DONOVAN: Evette—a charming name.

(DONOVAN *and* CLAIRE *shake hands.*)

TIM: Evette Giroux.

DONOVAN: Good heavens, that's a coincidence. I know another Evette Giroux. Needless to say, a French girl, too. Not nearly as pretty as you, though. (*Bows gallantly.*) Enchanté, madame. My great pleasure. Do you speak English?

TIM: She—

(CLAIRE *holds up her hand to silence* TIM. *Pause. Then:*)

CLAIRE: (*With French accent*) I understand perfectly.

DONOVAN: Of course you do; and if I may make so bold as to say so, you speak—

TIM: She doesn't understand you. 'I understand perfectly'— that's the only English she knows—just one phrase—only

33

one phrase—that's all she ever says—
(*Again* CLAIRE *silences him with her hand. Pause. Then:*)

CLAIRE: (*With French accent*) That is a lie.

TIM: Excellent, Evette! A second phrase! When did you learn that? Congratulations! Two phrases—deux phrases—excellent!

DONOVAN: And two such wonderful phrases—'I understand perfectly' and 'That is a lie'—a précis of life, aren't they?

TIM: She's a very clever lady, Evette. She learns very rapidly.

DONOVAN: When you're as young and as beautiful as Madame Giroux, language doesn't matter, does it? Words are superfluous, aren't they?

CLAIRE: I understand perfectly.

DONOVAN: Of course you do— (*pointing to his heart*)—here.

CLAIRE: Timothy . . .?

TIM: Yes?
(*She takes his arm, she has something private to say to him.*)

CLAIRE: Timothy—

TIM: It's time to go—is that it? That's fine—go ahead.

CLAIRE: No, no. Please, Timothy, mon . . . mon . . .
(*She tosses her head in frustration and points towards the clothes-line.*)

TIM: Thank you for all your good work. (*To* DONOVAN) She's a sort of caretaker—cleans the place for me. (*To* CLAIRE) See you next time I'm back, Evette. Tell Barney I was asking for him. (*To* DONOVAN) Man as communicator—doesn't always work, does it? I mean in a situation like this we can hardly explain the individual as being simultaneously creator and creation of his own communicational possibilities, can we?—ha-ha-ha.

CLAIRE: Timothy, please, mon . . . mon . . .
(*She leads him a few steps away. Now she attempts to mime her request—she touches her midriff with her fingertips.*)

TIM: Ah, you're thirsty! Can I get you a bowl of vodka?

DONOVAN: Perhaps I could help, Evette?

CLAIRE: No, no, Timothy only. Please, Timothy, mon . . . mon . . .
(*Again the mime.*)

34

TIM: I'm sorry. I just don't understand what—
CLAIRE: Ah!
> (*Suddenly her eyes light up. She sees the bra protruding from his pocket. She retrieves it and holds it up in triumph.*)
> Ah! Merci! Merci!
> (*She smiles sweetly, shyly, at both men and runs into the bedroom.*)
TIM: Ha–ha. I would never have got that. Never. I thought she was ravenous.
DONOVAN: Have you something to tell me, Tim?
TIM: I certainly have.
DONOVAN: I will not have my only child hurt, Tim.
TIM: Of course not. It's an ugly story.
DONOVAN: I'm listening.
TIM: (*Lowering his voice*) When her husband gets drunk, he beats her. He's an animal in drink. Only today he tried to drown her near the rocks at the far end of the beach. Artificial respiration; all that stuff. That's why my father gave her the key to this house—so that she can escape from him when things become unbearable. And that's why she insists on doing the housework—it makes her feel she's not a charity. It's the only dignity she has left.
DONOVAN: Why doesn't she report him?
TIM: She has—several times. But he's a very wealthy man— probably a millionaire. He has a lot of influence.
DONOVAN: Even with the authorities here?
TIM: Everywhere.
DONOVAN: You've met him?
TIM: Yes. Oh, yes. He torments me every time I come here.
DONOVAN: Torments you?
TIM: He wants to buy me out.
DONOVAN: This house?
TIM: House, land, the whole place. Offers me a fortune for it every weekend.
DONOVAN: This drunken German?
TIM: Hands me a blank cheque. He never gives up.
DONOVAN: Typical bloody German. Overrun you if you gave them half a chance. You're not selling to him, of course?

TIM: Never.

DONOVAN: Good man. I'm going to make some enquiries about our German friend.

SUSAN: (*Off*) Yo–ho! Yo–ho!

DONOVAN: Not a word of this to Susie. She's very sensitive. Stories like that affect her badly.

(SUSAN *enters carrying two small suitcases. She is in her early twenties, pert, pretty, assured. She is dressed in jeans and a blouse.*)

SUSAN: Shame on you, Timmy, having me carry these big things. They're a ton weight.

DONOVAN: No, they're not.

TIM: I'm sorry. I didn't—

SUSAN: And shame on you, too, Daddy.

DONOVAN: Don't listen to her.

(*She leaves the cases in the centre of the floor and kisses* TIM *lightly on the cheek.*)

SUSAN: Hello, you.

TIM: Hello, Susan.

DONOVAN: I was just saying I'm delighted we made the detour. It's a very special place, isn't it?

SUSAN: (*Looking around*) I love it—I love it—I love it. Don't you love it, Daddy? Isn't it just unbelievable? I think it's just unbelievable.

DONOVAN: I'm going to have a look around. How much land do you own?

TIM: All you can see.

DONOVAN: Really? Splendid. I've a speech to mull over. I'll be back soon.

(*He leaves and closes both doors behind him.*)

SUSAN: How are you? Are we very evil deceiving poor Daddy like this? No, we're not. We're just naughty. What did he say? Was he impressed? What does he think?

TIM: He thinks it's unbelievable.

SUSAN: Terrific. That's very important to us. And he's very knowledgeable about old ruins. And you look so miserable.

TIM: Do I?

(*She throws her arms around him and gives him a long kiss. As*

36

before his concern is CLAIRE's *whereabouts.*)

SUSAN: Are you glad to see me?

TIM: Indeed.

SUSAN: 'Indeed'! Say it then.

TIM: I'm glad to see you.

SUSAN: How glad? Tell me how glad.

TIM: A very, very large quantity of glad indeed.

SUSAN: You're quaint—that's what you are. And I've a crow to pick with you, Timmy Sly Boots.

TIM: What crow is that?

SUSAN: You never told me you'd bought a motorbike.

TIM: Me?

SUSAN: A big, old Honda. At the side of the house.

TIM: Oh, that—that's not mine.

SUSAN: Whose is it?

TIM: I have the use of it all right but I don't own it. It belongs to a friend of mine. A local. A neighbour.

SUSAN: Who is he?

TIM: He's a woman. Nora Dan. Nora the Scrambler. She lets me have it to go scrambling on the sand-dunes.

SUSAN: She scrambles herself, this Nora Dan?

TIM: Brilliant at it. Donegal champion.

SUSAN: Is she young?

TIM: Ex-champion. She's not so young now.

SUSAN: Will you take me out? Please, Timmy! I'd love to go scrambling.

TIM: Any time at all. Of course.

SUSAN: Now?!

TIM: After a while—after you've seen around. How long can you stay? (*Indicating the cases*) What are these for?

SUSAN: Our dress clothes for the damned dinner in Sligo this evening. But I was thinking, now that Daddy adores this place, I'll try to persuade him to drive back home this way tomorrow morning and maybe even spend the weekend here. Wouldn't that be unbelievable?

TIM: Indeed.

SUSAN: Whatever about this damned house, I would have made him bring me here today just so that I could see you.

TIM: Yes.

SUSAN: Kiss me, Timmy.

TIM: Yes.

(*Again she flings her arms around him and kisses him.*)

SUSAN: (*Dreamily*) If you only had a job, we could make real plans, Timmy.

TIM: I have a job.

SUSAN: Not a real job. I mean they could kick you out any second, couldn't they?

TIM: I suppose so.

SUSAN: And where would we be then? And I was thinking that if you were to talk to Daddy—

(*She breaks off suddenly, because, looking over TIM's shoulder, she sees the yellow pants on the clothes-line.*)

What's that, Timmy?

TIM: What?

SUSAN: Who else is in the house?

TIM: Nobody. What do you mean?

SUSAN: Whose are those on the clothes-line?

TIM: Those? Oh, those are mine.

SUSAN: They're not!

TIM: They are.

SUSAN: That colour?!

TIM: That's my lucky colour.

SUSAN: Oh, you are a devil.

TIM: They must be dry by now.

(*He rushes to the line, grabs the pants and stuffs them into his pocket.*)

Now. You'll want to get changed. Which case is yours?

SUSAN: The blue one. What's the rush?

TIM: Just to get things organized a bit. Time's running out. The blue one it is. Fine. Up we go. I'll lead the way.

(*He goes up the stairs.* SUSAN *follows him.*)

So it's a dress affair tonight?

(*As they go upstairs* CLAIRE *enters from the bedroom and hangs a waistslip on the line.*)

SUSAN: Boring.

TIM: And there'll be speeches?

SUSAN: Scores of them.

TIM: Wonderful. You'll enjoy that. Dress speeches and scores of dinners. Here we are—in there. I'll see you downstairs.

SUSAN: Timmy.

(*She kisses her fingertips and places them on his lips.*)

TIM: See you when you're ready.

(*She goes into the loft bedroom. He dashes downstairs and straight to the bedroom door. He flings it open and throws the pants inside.*)

(*Frantic whisper*) I'm warning you, Claire! Get to hell out of here now or I'll break your bloody neck!

CLAIRE: Oh, you are a devil. Why don't you get a real job?

(*The voice comes from behind him. He wheels round—*CLAIRE *is sitting on the settle bed.*)

TIM: I'm warning you—

CLAIRE: Daddy could get you a real job. He's on the governing body.

TIM: You know what you're doing, don't you?

(SUSAN's *head appears over the rail.*)

SUSAN: Timmy, have you an iron?

(*He pulls the curtains across the settle bed.*)

TIM: Have I an iron what?

CLAIRE: (*Behind curtain*) A smoothing iron, you eejit!

TIM: Oh, a smoothing iron? Sorry. Sorry.

SUSAN: Doesn't matter. I'll just hang this dress up for a while.

(*She withdraws.*)

CLAIRE: What would she plug it into?—the thatch? But you were going to tell me what I'm doing to you.

(*He finds his bowl and pours himself another drink.*)

TIM: You're doing two things to me. Not only are you ensuring I won't get tenure but that I may even lose the bloody miserable job.

(SUSAN's *head appears again.*)

SUSAN: Are you talking to somebody, Timmy?

TIM: Just to myself. Preparing a lecture.

SUSAN: You're quaint. And unique. And mine.

(*She blows a kiss and withdraws.*)

CLAIRE: 'And mine.'

39

TIM: And secondly—secondly—in the space of half an hour you've succeeded in changing the—the—the very high regard I've had for you for a long, long time—

CLAIRE: Regard? Hah!

TIM: —into—into—into bloody hatred of you.
(CLAIRE *sticks her head out.*)

CLAIRE: If you ever had any regard—as you call it—for me, you certainly succeeded in concealing it from me!
(*The big door suddenly blows open.* CLAIRE's *head disappears.*)
What was that?

TIM: That damned door. It does that all the time.

CLAIRE: The latch is faulty.

TIM: I know.

CLAIRE: Last night about midnight—Nora Dan and I had been sitting chatting and she had just left—I was about to go to bed when suddenly the door burst open and blew out the lamp. Then of course I thought I heard footsteps. And there I was in the pitch black, on the point of tears and groping about for matches. I didn't sleep until morning.

TIM: Were you frightened?

CLAIRE: Terrified.

TIM: I'm sure. Did you ever have a sense that a place hates you? —that it actually feels malevolent towards you? I think this house hates me. I'm convinced that the genii of this house detest me.

CLAIRE: 'This shaped all our souls.'

TIM: Did you hear me? God, I'm ashamed of myself. But I'm serious about this place. Maybe it's because I feel no affinity at all with it and it knows that. In fact I think I hate it and all it represents. And it senses that. And that's why it's out to get me. D'you see that fireplace? Every time I go near that damned hearth it attacks me—spews its filthy smoke all over me. Maybe it's not malign in itself but it's the willing, the conniving instrument of a malign presence.

CLAIRE: (*Laughs.*) Rubbish!

TIM: Right. Right. Just watch. Are you watching?
(*Her head appears.*)

CLAIRE: Yes.

(*He looks at the fireplace. Panic—he sees the slip on the line.*)

TIM: Where did that—?! You're the malign spirit! I'll get you for this, Claire!

(*He dashes to the fireplace and grabs the slip. The smoke bellows and envelops him.*)

O my God.

(CLAIRE *exits by the front door. He is spluttering, wiping his eyes, etc. when* NORA DAN *enters. He sticks the slip into his pocket.*)

NORA: Don't cut it until it cools down a bit. But maybe you don't care for homemade bread, do you?

TIM: Thank you very much. I love it.

NORA: You love it surely. And you have a bit of reek? Ah sure that aul chimney never pulled right. Sure this aul house is only a byre by right. People with any self-respect wouldn't live in it. Give some of this to Claire—she likes it, too. Is she about?

TIM: She's having a sleep. She was awake all night.

NORA: Was she, the creature? She's tired so.

TIM: Claire.

NORA: Let her be if she's—

TIM: She's awake now. Claire, it's— (*He pulls back the curtains. She is not there. The usual panic—where is she now?*)
She was there a second ago.

NORA: And I see Jack out swimming in the tide. Lord, the comings and goings there is about the place! Weeks, months maybe, and sure we don't see a soul; and then all of a sudden the place is throng. There's a fine big gentleman out walking the fields, the one that left his car down at the road. Oh, the man that owns that big car, that's the man with the money. Who would he be?

(TIM *has been looking into the bedroom, up the stairs, out of the door—where is she now?*)

TIM: Dr Donovan.

NORA: He is indeed.

TIM: He's a senator, too.

NORA: A senator, too. Two big jobs. Wouldn't you know it to

look at him. And the girl that's with him—she'll be his daughter?

TIM: That's right. That's Susan.

NORA: Susan surely. There you are. Oh, they'll be the bucks with the money. And what do they make of a poor, backward place like this?

TIM: They think it's unbelievable.

NORA: They do surely, the poor creatures. Ah, sure for all their money people like that have no sense at all.

(DONOVAN *enters energetically.*)

DONOVAN: That was good. I needed that. I'm restored now. (*To* NORA) Hello.

TIM: This is Dr Donovan. Nora Dan—a neighbour of mine.

DONOVAN: How are you?

NORA: You're welcome, Doctor, welcome.

DONOVAN: Thank you very much. May I tell you something, Nora Dan? You are a privileged woman living in a place like this.

NORA: I am surely, Doctor.

DONOVAN: Privileged and blessed. Treasure it, Nora. Cherish it. (*Taking* TIM *aside*) I'll be speaking to the Chief Superintendent tonight. I'll mention that case to him.

TIM: Case?

DONOVAN: The battered wife—that French girl, Evette. Is Giroux her married name?

TIM: It's her maiden name.

DONOVAN: What's the husband's name, the German thug?

TIM: Munich. Herr Munich.

DONOVAN: Did you say Barney?

TIM: That's right. Herr Barney Munich.

DONOVAN: Fine. Leave it with me. (*Aloud*) Forgive me, Nora. A small act of charity to atone for my sins. There's a young man having the time of his life swimming down there.

NORA: That's Jack. His people live in—

TIM: He's a local. A fisherman. We call him Jack the Cod.

DONOVAN: Jack the Cod! I love that. Call a man Jack the Cod and you tell me his name and his profession and that he's not very good at his profession. Concise, accurate and nicely malicious. Beautiful! Tell me, Nora, what would be the chances of picking up a cottage around here? Or even a site?

NORA: Ah, sure what would a gentleman like you want with a place here?

DONOVAN: Renewal, Nora. Restoration. Fulfilment. Back to the true centre.

NORA: The true centre surely.

DONOVAN: Would there be anything on the market?

NORA: Sure I can ask around.

DONOVAN: Would you?

NORA: A place about this size, maybe?

DONOVAN: Ideal. There's just my daughter and myself.

NORA: And not too dear. Surely, Doctor, I'll ask around.

DONOVAN: You're a great woman.

(SUSAN *comes downstairs in a dressing-gown. She has a towel in her hand.*)

SUSAN: The comb must be in your case, Daddy. (*To* NORA) Hello.

DONOVAN: My daughter, Susie.

NORA: You're very welcome.

(SUSAN *leaves the towel across the back of a chair.*)

DONOVAN: This splendid lady lives here. Nora Dan.

SUSAN: Nora Dan?

NORA: Nora Dan surely.

SUSAN: You're the scrambler! She scrambles, Daddy!

DONOVAN: She what?

SUSAN: She goes scrambling on the sand-dunes! (*To* NORA) Isn't that true? (*To* DONOVAN) She's Nora the Scrambler!

DONOVAN: Jack the Cod I got instantly but Nora the Scrambler. . . . Give me a clue. Has it to do with eggs? You keep hens!

NORA: I keep hens surely.

DONOVAN: There! Beautiful!

NORA: I have three.

SUSAN: Daddy, you fool, I'm talking about motorbikes!

DONOVAN: What motorbikes?

SUSAN: Who's she?

43

(CLAIRE *has entered carrying an armful of turf which she deposits into the creel.*)

TIM: Thank you very much. That's fine. Just throw it there. Off you go.

SUSAN: Who's that?

NORA: (*To* DONOVAN) If I have any news for you, Doctor, I'll be straight back. (*As she passes* CLAIRE) You're the better of that wee sleep. You're looking grand now.
(*She leaves.*)

TIM: That's all for today. Thank you very much.

CLAIRE: That is a lie.

SUSAN: Who is that woman, Daddy?

DONOVAN: Shhh. Sordid story. Tell you later.

SUSAN: Is she a foreigner?

TIM: That's everything now, Evette. Nothing more for you to do, thank you.

SUSAN: (*To* DONOVAN) Evette?

TIM: I can manage everything else myself now.

SUSAN: I want to know. Who is that woman?

DONOVAN: Shhh. (*To* CLAIRE) Pardonnez-moi, Madame, I—will —help—you. I—understand—perfectly.

SUSAN: I don't understand at all! Who is this woman, Timmy?
(CLAIRE *is now standing in front of* TIM: *and as before she begins to mime. She points towards the fireplace and then strokes her legs and thighs.*)

CLAIRE: Timothy, please, please, mon . . .

SUSAN: Why doesn't she speak English?

DONOVAN: She's French, darling; married to a German.

SUSAN: What the hell does she want?

TIM: Go on. Out you get. That's all for today. Off you go.

CLAIRE: Mon . . . please, Timothy . . . mon . . .

SUSAN: I heard her speaking English!
(TIM'*s panic and confusion suddenly endow him with a desperate authority. He grabs* CLAIRE *by the arm and marches her to the door.*)

TIM: Didn't you hear what I said? I said that's all for today. The house is spotless. All the work is done.

CLAIRE: Please, Timothy, please . . .

44

TIM: (*To* DONOVAN) Wouldn't be difficult to analyse this discourse, Doctor?—ha–ha–ha.

SUSAN: Is he drunk?

TIM: Off you go to your caravan, thank you very much. Your husband will be waiting for you. You'll have a meal to make for him. I'll see you the next time I'm here. (*He has pushed her outside the house and closes the half-door behind her.*)

CLAIRE: Please, Timothy—

TIM: No please Timothy about it. I've been more than patient with you.

CLAIRE: Ah!
(*She has spotted the slip in his pocket. She reaches across the door, retrieves it and, as before, holds it up in triumph.*)
Merci, Timothy. Merci.
(*She runs away.* TIM *is momentarily at a loss. All he can do is brazen it out and continue to parade his bogus authority.*)

SUSAN: That was her slip, Timmy!

TIM: Yes, that was her slip and I had it in my pocket.

SUSAN: You—

TIM: And why was it in my pocket? I will tell you why it was in my pocket. When she comes in to clean the house I allow her to do her own washing here because she lives in a caravan that has no light and no running water—

SUSAN: But you have—

TIM: —and when she finishes her washing she hangs her things on that line there even though she knows that the damned fire smokes and ruins her wash. And so just because she's a stupid and a stubborn bitch and almost certainly animated by some inexplicable spite against me, what I have to do is run around after her and pull the things off the line and hang them on the backs of chairs. Look. (*Points to* SUSAN's *towel across a chair.*) That's what I have to do.

SUSAN: Timmy, that's mine. I left it there.

TIM: Of course you left it there because it wouldn't fit into my pocket, would it? Right. You want to change, Doctor, don't you? In there, if you please.
(*Hands* DONOVAN *his case and indicates the bedroom.*)

45

And you want a comb, Susan? (*Produces one from his pocket.*) There you are. One comb. And even though the company's good, time is running out and you've got to be in Sligo by six which means that you have got to be out of this house in five minutes at the very outside. Right?

DONOVAN: (*Looking at his watch*) God, is that the time? You're right, Tim. We ought to get a move on.

TIM: It occurred to me, Doctor, when you were asking Nora Dan about buying a site here, it occurred to me and I'm sure the thought crossed your own mind, too: what about one of my sites?

DONOVAN: Actually that did cross my mind but I—

TIM: Of course it did. Why wouldn't it? I'll tell you what: get yourself dressed up and we'll talk business then. All right?

DONOVAN: Indeed. Excellent. You've no idea, Susie, how special, how very special all this is to me. See those posts and chains over there? Haven't seen those since I was a child. I'll explain them to you before we leave. You're right, Tim, absolutely right. This is the true centre.

(DONOVAN *goes into the bedroom,* SUSAN *stares at* TIM *in amazement.*)

TIM: An interesting discourse phenomenon that. Called statement transference. I never used the phrase 'This is the true centre' but by imputing the phrase to me, as the Doctor has just done, he both seeks confirmation for his own sentiments and suggests to listeners outside the duologue that he and I are unanimous in that sentiment ... which we're not ... (*His bogus authority suddenly deserts him.*) ... not at all ... O my God ... where's my bowl of vodka?

SUSAN: Timmy, are you not well?

TIM: I left a drink somewhere.

SUSAN: This isn't your house, Timmy. You have no sites for sale.

TIM: Where did I put it?

SUSAN: And there is no running water in this house. And that—that—that French woman, whoever she is, what is she doing here with you?

46

TIM: I thought I left it there.

(DONOVAN *emerges from the bedroom with the yellow pants in his hand.*)

DONOVAN: Sorry. I think these must be . . .

(TIM *takes them from him.*)

TIM: Thank you very much, Doctor. I was just looking for them.

(DONOVAN *exits. Aware of* SUSAN'*s very cold eye on him,* TIM *does not know what to do with the pants. He begins to stuff them into one pocket. No, not that. He looks at the line. No, not that. He begins to stuff them into the other pocket.*)

SUSAN: They're your own, aren't they? Why don't you just put them on?

TIM: They're damp.

SUSAN: You and I are going to have a business chat, too, Timmy.

TIM: Certainly. Any time that suits you.

SUSAN: And that bloody fire doesn't smoke either!

TIM: It doesn't smoke, does it not? You just watch this. Do you see that fire? That fire loathes me!

(*He goes to the fireplace and stares challengingly at it. Nothing happens. Still staring at it he takes the pants from his pocket and drapes them on the line. Nothing happens.*)

SUSAN: Liar!

TIM: True as God, every other time I did that, Susan, honest to God—

(*The sudden blow-down with the usual consequences. He snatches the pants off the line.*)

O my God.

SUSAN: I hope it chokes you.

(*She runs upstairs.*

He goes through the usual routine with his glasses, etc. When he has recovered he goes to the dresser to refill his bowl.

BARNEY THE BANKS, *the German, enters. As Nora Dan has said, he is about the same age and build as Jack; and he is apt to gulder.* TIM, *who has not yet put on his glasses, assumes he is Jack.*)

BARNEY: Ah—hello! Finally we encounter—ja? At long length.

TIM: Oh—hello. (*Softly*) I told you it wouldn't work, you

47

bastard you. (*Loudly*) Isn't it a beautiful day?

BARNEY: Ja, ja. Beautiful. Beautiful.

(*With both arms fully outstretched and using the index finger of both hands as pointers,* TIM *signals to the bedroom and to the loft to indicate where* DONOVAN *and* SUSAN *are.*)

TIM: (*Softly*) Doctor. Susan. Doctor. Susan.

BARNEY: I know you are here since I see the motorbike parking outside.

TIM: Yes, parking away there. (*Softly*) It's all falling apart. (*Pointing again*) Doctor. Susan. (*Loudly*) Welcome.

(BARNEY, *at first puzzled but now assuming that the outstretched arms and the upturned index fingers must be some form of local greeting, now laughs and copies the gesture.*)

BARNEY: Welcome? Ah, ja, ja, ja! Welcome! Danke schön—thank you. And to you also. Welcome home to handsome Ballybeg. (*Slight bow.*) My name is Willie—

TIM: (*Softly*) Munich—Munich—Munich—Willie Munich. (*Loudly*) Good to see you again, Willie. (*Remembering; softly*) No, it's not Willie—it's Barney—Barney—Barney Munich. (*Loudly*) How have you been keeping, Barney? (*Softly*) God, I think I'm going off my head.

BARNEY: Going where? Leaving, ja?

TIM: (*Softly*) D'you know what I've just done? I've practically sold one of your father's fields to Dr Bollocks!

BARNEY: Dr Bollocks? He is selling—?

TIM: (*Softly*) Shhh. And Claire's doing her damnedest to ruin me. Oh, I'll get her, all right! But Susan smells a rat. Susan's no fool.

BARNEY: (*Matching* TIM'*s soft tone*) You talk too fast for—

TIM: (*Softly*) Gulder, man! You're supposed to gulder! (*Loudly*) This is our first cathedral, isn't it? The question is: are we worthy of it? (*Softly*) D'you know what she wants me to do? Take her scrambling! On Nora Dan's motorbike!

BARNEY: Nora Dan?

TIM: (*Softly*) Yes, yours! All right! But I can't even ride a push-bike!

BARNEY: Ja, ja, I understand Nora Dan good. But you talk quick, too quick for me.

TIM: (*Loudly*) I beg your pardon, Barney. I'll slow down.

(*Softly and very rapidly*) Listen carefully, Jack. You're a German thug called Barney Munich and you're married to Claire Harkin whose real name is Evette Giroux. You drink like a fish and beat the tar out of her and he's going to have you arrested. (*Loudly*) Yes, yes, this is indeed the true centre. (*Softly and very rapidly*) In real life you're Jack the Cod, a local fisherman, an eejit—he spotted you out swimming. And I let your wife, Evette Giroux—in real life, Claire—I let her do her washing here because you have no running water in the caravan and I have here—even though in fact I haven't—but I think he hasn't noticed though sly puss Susan has. (*Loudly*) But if not the true centre, perhaps the true off-centre. Most definitely the true off-centre. (*Softly and very rapidly*) And I own all the land you can see around here and if Susan has her way they'll come back here tomorrow and spend the weekend here and even if I can talk her out of taking her scrambling today, she'll make sure I break my bloody neck at it tomorrow. And your wife persists in leaving her wet clothes on the line even though that damned fire smokes although it smokes only on me and nobody else but that's because it hates me and I hate it, hate the whole damned place, and I've got to go round after her, picking them up— (*Produces the pants from his pocket.*) Look! Your wife's!

(*All of this speech has been delivered urgently into* THE GERMAN's *ear.* THE GERMAN *has retreated before it and* TIM *has pursued him.* THE GERMAN *is now quite nervous. He finds himself up against the door-frame and feels around for a defensive implement. His hand finds the flail. Now* TIM *thrusts the pants into his hands—so* THE GERMAN *now has the pants in one hand and the flail in the other.*)

And now, I suppose, we're going to have your special Donegal midsummer orgy! Terrific, my friend! You have a wonderful sense of humour! (*Totally defeated he slumps into a chair.*) O my God, it's out of hand, Jack! I can't go on! It's all in pieces.

BARNEY: (*Stiffly*) I come here just to talk to you business, Herr

McNeilis, and not to—

TIM: (*Suddenly impassioned again; shouts*) You're McNeilis!
(*Softly*) You're McNeilis. I'm Gallagher—Gallagher—
Gallagher!
(*And with both index fingers he jabs at his temple each time he
says the word 'Gallagher'.*)

BARNEY: (*Copying the gesture*) Gallagher—ja?

TIM: Yes. Ja. Gallagher. Gallagher. Tim Gallagher—isn't it? I
hardly know myself. God, Jack, get me a drink. There's
vodka over there.

BARNEY: Vodka? Ah—vodka! Danke schön. I like little vodka.
Thank you. You are kind. Where is vodka?

TIM: On the dresser.

BARNEY: Sorry?

TIM: Gulder.

BARNEY: The gulder?—(*finds the bottle*)—ah, the gulder, yes. It is
a handsome gulder, too. I like it.

TIM: What are you raving about, Jack?

BARNEY: I come here to talk to you business, Herr McNeilis.
But some other day. I write you letter three times from the
address Nora Dan give me because I wish to sell this house
from you. Are you receiving my letter?

TIM: (*Wearily*) Yes . . . yes . . .

BARNEY: That is good.
(BARNEY *hands* TIM *a bowl of vodka and has a bowl himself.*)
Vodka is handsome. Ah—I learn a toast from this English
book I read last night. What is it? Ja, I know. (*Bowl in one
hand, pants in the other; both raised:*) 'To us lovers
everywhere!'

TIM: (*Wearily*) Cut it out, Jack.
(DONOVAN *enters. He is now wearing his dress suit.*)

BARNEY: Good? Ja? 'To us lovers everywhere!'

DONOVAN: It looks as if this is not the right moment.

TIM: Doctor, this is—this is Barney Munich, the German I
mentioned to you.

DONOVAN: I guessed as much.

TIM: (*Whispers to* DONOVAN) He's on the bottle. Careful.

BARNEY: (*Slight bow.*) My name is Willie Hausenbach.

DONOVAN: It certainly is not.

BARNEY: Welcome to handsome Ballybeg, Dr Bollocks.

(And as before BARNEY *stretches his arms out, as he has learned from* TIM; *index fingers pointing upwards, arms waving up and down in the welcome gesture.)*

TIM: Christ, Jack—! *(Suddenly realizing)* Christ, it's not—

DONOVAN: My name, sir, happens to be Donovan. Dr Donovan. Senator Donovan.

TIM: *(To* DONOVAN*)* He's drunk. He's violent. Humour him.

BARNEY: I am sorry—my English it is too bad. You are a doctor of medicine?

DONOVAN: I am.

BARNEY: May I speak private to you, Doctor?

DONOVAN: I'd prefer if you didn't.

BARNEY: *(Whispering)* May I say to you, Doctor, I think your friend, Herr McNeilis, is—

DONOVAN: Gallagher?

BARNEY: Correct, Doctor. Correct. *(Touching his head)* Just a little bit gallagher. He says himself so to me. He tells me, 'I'm gallagher–gallagher–gallagher.' So we take care, Doctor—ja? We talk to him soft—ja? *(Aloud)* I come to speak to Herr McNeilis to buy his house to me because I love it so. But perhaps some other day—

*(*SUSAN *in formal dress is coming down the stairs.)*

DONOVAN: Go back up, Susie, please. *(To* BARNEY*)* What were you saying?

*(*SUSAN *continues down.)*

BARNEY: I say I speak to your friend some other day perhaps when he is not so—not so frisky. Please to give him this.

(He hands the pants to DONOVAN.*)*

DONOVAN: What's this?

BARNEY: Thank you.

DONOVAN: These are Mrs Munich's.

(He hands them back to BARNEY.*)*

TIM: *(To* DONOVAN*)* Don't anger him.

BARNEY: Mrs—? Ah, your wife.

DONOVAN: Susie is my daughter.

BARNEY: *(Bows.)* Handsome daughter. Fräulein Bollocks.

(BARNEY *hands the pants to* SUSAN.)

SUSAN: They aren't mine! They're his! (TIM's)

DONOVAN: Tim's?

SUSAN: Yes!

DONOVAN: How do you know?

(SUSAN *hands the pants to* TIM.)

SUSAN: They're perfectly dry now!

BARNEY: (*To* SUSAN) Welcome to handsome Ballybeg.

(*And again he mimes the welcome gesture.*)

TIM: Careful—he's getting madder.

SUSAN: God, he's obscene! (BARNEY)

BARNEY: Ja, Ja, very, very.

TIM: D'you see?

SUSAN: Timmy, whose are they?

TIM: Evette's.

SUSAN: That French tramp?

TIM: His wife's.

(TIM *hands the pants to* BARNEY.)

DONOVAN: Tim's right.

SUSAN: How do you know?

DONOVAN: He told me.

SUSAN: (*To* BARNEY) Your—wife—is—called—Evette?

BARNEY: Ah. Ja–ja–ja–ja. Evette. (*Bows again.*) Welcome,
Evette.

DONOVAN: Of course she's called Evette.

SUSAN: (*To* TIM) And how did you get them?

TIM: I had them in my pocket. Your father was there. He saw it
all.

SUSAN: (*To* DONOVAN) You were there?

TIM: No, I'm wrong. He was only there for the . . .
(*He imitates* CLAIRE's *bra mime.*)

DONOVAN: That'll do–that'll do–that'll do! I am not going to
argue any longer with a drunkard, a wife-beater, and very
probably a man of unnatural vice.

BARNEY: Thank you, Doctor.

DONOVAN: And I will make it my business this very evening to
see that an end is put to his vile gallop. Those are the
property of your unfortunate wife, sir.

52

BARNEY: Perhaps I—

DONOVAN: And please leave this decent Irish home immediately. You are going to learn very soon, my friend, that there are still places in this world, little pockets of decency and decorum, where your wealth means nothing at all.

BARNEY: (*Puzzled*) I leave them on the gulder for when he is not so gallagher.

(NORA DAN *enters*.)

NORA: I just remembered, Doctor: there's a site near the main road that might suit you; but the man that owns it is away in the town today. Oh, Lord, but you're looking swanky, Doctor!

DONOVAN: Thank you, Nora.

NORA: And Susan! Oh dear, oh dear, you're beau–ti–ful. Isn't that (*dress*) lovely. You paid a big penny for that. Oh, yous'll stand out, the pair of you, with all those big toffs tonight. And Barney! How are you, Barney?

BARNEY: Good, Nora, thank you.

NORA: Isn't she just beau–ti–ful?

BARNEY: Fräulein Evette? Ja, ja, beau–ti–ful.

NORA: Would you look at the eyes of him, Doctor! He'll be off with her before you know.

DONOVAN: (*Taking* NORA *aside*) Nora, a moment, please.

SUSAN: I want to talk to you before I leave, Timmy.

TIM: Certainly.

DONOVAN: The balance is very delicate, Nora. Don't trifle with him.

NORA: Is it Barney the Banks?

DONOVAN: Is that what you call him? Of course—because of his wealth! Well-named indeed. But be careful, Nora. Unsavoury material that.

NORA: Unsavoury surely, Doctor.

DONOVAN: I'll talk to the Chief Superintendent about him tonight. Now about that business of the site: don't bother pursuing that, thank you all the same.

NORA: Sure I knew that a gentleman like yourself wouldn't want to live in a backward place like this.

DONOVAN: Tim has made me an offer.

NORA: Tim?

DONOVAN: Maybe his own place here. Not a word.

NORA: He's selling you this house?

DONOVAN: Shh. Or at least a site. I don't want to rush him.

BARNEY: Well, please, I think I leave now. Goodbye. (*To* TIM)
Again perhaps we will talk at long length. Nora.

NORA: I'll see you later, Barney.

BARNEY: Please, yes. (*To* SUSAN) Auf Wiedersehen, Evette.
(*He leaves. The big door is left open, the half-door shut.*)

SUSAN: I'm leaving now, Daddy.

DONOVAN: Come here till I show you these first, Susie (*the posts
and chains*). Brilliant idea to retain them, Tim. Look,
Susie. What happened was this. I drive my cow through the
door here—or my two cows if I'm a man of substance.

NORA: A man of substance indeed.

DONOVAN: There was an old Irish expression for that, wasn't
there? What was it?—'as rich as a woman with two cows'—
wasn't that it? Now, if our little scenario takes place in, say,
the early nineteenth century, then our fireplace will be there
(*centre of the floor*) with the smoke going straight up
through a hole in the roof; and that is why the modest but
aesthetically satisfying furnishings in the traditional Irish
kitchen are always placed along the walls, leaving this area
completely free for moving around.
(*All eyes are on* THE DOCTOR *when* JACK *appears at the
half-door—pretending he is the German. Only* TIM *sees him.
Throughout part of* DONOVAN'*s monologue* TIM *and* JACK
mime the following exchange:
    JACK: *I'm the German. I'm coming in. Okay?*
    TIM: *No, no. Go away. Go away.*
    JACK: *What's wrong? I love your house. I want to buy it.*
    TIM: *For God's sake—go! The German was here.*
    JACK: *Look. My cheque book. My pen. What money do you
        want?*
    TIM: *Please, Jack! Go away!*
    JACK: *And look at the time! Your time is up!*
    TIM: *Please!*)

NORA: Moving around surely, Doctor.

DONOVAN: But let's bring our little scenario forward in time, let's say to the turn of the century. Right. The fireplace has moved up to the gable. This is now the heart of the home. That's where we warm ourselves. That's where we cook. That's where we kneel and pray. That's where we gather at night to tell our folk tales and our ancient sagas. Correct, Tim?

TIM: Our ancient sagas surely, Doctor.

(At the very end of the mime above, SUSAN happens to glance at TIM. JACK immediately crouches down behind the half-door. But TIM is caught making his final impassioned 'Please!'. Aware that SUSAN is now looking at him, he converts the gesture into blowing a kiss to her.)

DONOVAN: So let us imagine it is night-time. Granny is asleep in the settle bed. My wife is knitting by the fireside, the children in a circle at her feet. I enter with my most valuable worldly possession—my cow! She knows the routine perfectly. With her slow and assured gait she crosses over there and stands waiting for me with her head beside the post where I have already placed a battle of hay. An interesting word that—'battle'—it must be Irish, Tim?

TIM: Scottish. Sixteenth century.

DONOVAN: Is it? Anyhow. I pick up my milking pail and my milking stool and I join her. I lift up the chain—(*he demonstrates*)—and bring it gently round her neck and secure it with the little clasp here—like this. Then I milk her. And when I'm finished, she'll stand here for another hour, perhaps two hours, just chewing her cud and listening to the reassuring sounds of a family preparing to go to bed. Then she will lie down and go to sleep. A magical scene, isn't it? It's a little scene that's somehow central to my psyche.

NORA: You're as good as a concert, Doctor. Isn't he?

SUSAN: Come on, Daddy. You're going to miss that dinner.

NORA: Sure they'll keep it warm for you, won't they? (*Going to the door*) Aren't the days getting very short?

(SUSAN goes towards the stairs.)

TIM: Let me get your case.

55

SUSAN: I can manage.

NORA: (*Looking out*) Barney the Banks is a very smart man on his feet. The lights are on in his caravan already.

SUSAN: (*To Tim*) 'No light and no running water'—hah!

TIM: Susan, I've got to explain to you—

SUSAN: I don't think you can—even if you were sober.

TIM: When I was at the door there, waving, that was to keep Jack McNeilis out.

DONOVAN: (*Tentatively*) Tim . . .?

SUSAN: He's here?

TIM: Yes.

SUSAN: What for?

TIM: He's somewhere out there waving his cheque book because time's running out.

DONOVAN: Can you come here for a minute, Tim?

TIM: Coming, Doctor.

SUSAN: His cheque book?

TIM: He wants to buy this house.

SUSAN: Why would he buy his own house?

TIM: Because he's a German. Don't move.

(*He dashes over to* THE DOCTOR *who is squatting on the ground —as he demonstrated—and chained to a post. Whether he is crouching down or standing up (never to his full height) he is chained in such a way that he is locked into a position facing the wall. Only with great difficulty and pain can he see over his shoulder—and then only a portion of the kitchen.*)

DONOVAN: Damned stupid of me. Don't seem to be able to get this clasp opened.

(TIM *crouches down beside him.*)

TIM: Is this it?

DONOVAN: Press it and it should open.

TIM: No.

DONOVAN: No—what?

TIM: The spring's broken. It's stuck.

DONOVAN: It was working perfectly a second ago.

TIM: It's getting dark in here. Maybe if you stood up . . .

(*They rise together.*)

SUSAN: Are you coming, Daddy?

56

DONOVAN: That is not a very intelligent question, darling, is it?
—Am I coming when I'm demonstrably stationary. (*To*
TIM) Are you attempting to choke me?

TIM: Sorry. I was only—

DONOVAN: Nora Dan!

NORA: What is it, Doctor?
(*She goes to him.*)

DONOVAN: (*To* TIM) Stand back, will you, please, and let Nora
Dan open it. (*To* NORA) Would you open that clip, please.

NORA: Open it surely, Doctor.
(*SUSAN runs upstairs. Now* TIM, NORA DAN *and* THE DOCTOR *are
in a huddle together.*)
Now—let me see. What did you do, Doctor?

DONOVAN: Isn't it apparent that I have secured myself to this
post?

NORA: You have surely. And that aul chain's that dirty and
rusty it has your good suit ruined. Wait till I wipe—
(*She begins dusting him vigorously.*)

DONOVAN: Never—never—never mind the clothes! Just open the
clasp!

TIM: You press that lever.

NORA: What lever?

TIM: That thing there.

NORA: Sure I haven't had a cow this forty years. It's terrible
dark here. (*To* TIM) Would you light the lamp?

TIM: Yes.
(*TIM goes to the table and lights the lamp. As he does:*)

NORA: You're grand, Doctor. Just grand. We'll have you free in
a minute. Sure this is no place for a gentleman like
yourself, tethered there like a brute beast.

DONOVAN: I'm quite comfortable actually except when I—when
I try to see over—

NORA: Don't stir yourself. Just stand still. Sure how can we milk
you if you start kicking and flicking your tail about—
ha–ha–ha.

DONOVAN: Ha–ha–ha.
(*TIM has lit the lamp and is about to lift it off the table when
CLAIRE, serene and smiling, enters, closing both doors behind her.*)

57

TIM: O my God.

CLAIRE: (*Softly, as she passes him*) I understand perfectly.
(*And without stopping she crosses the floor and goes into the
bedroom. Just as she is about to enter the bedroom,* SUSAN
*emerges from the loft with her case. She gets a glimpse of a
figure disappearing into the bedroom and she dashes down the
stairs.*)

NORA: Bring it over here, Tim.

TIM: Coming—coming.

SUSAN: Somebody's just gone into that room!

NORA: That's grand. Now we'll see what we're at.

SUSAN: It's that French tramp! She's back!

NORA: What's that?

TIM: (*Sings*) 'When the lights go on again . . .'

DONOVAN: It's not exactly a celebration, Tim, is it?

SUSAN: She's in there! I saw her! She's in there now!

NORA: Now I can see. Hold it steady there, Tim.

TIM: All right?

NORA: It's that wee clasp surely. God bless us and save us, I
can't get a budge out of it.
(SUSAN *drops her case in the middle of the floor and proclaims:*)

SUSAN: That French tramp is in that bedroom! What is that
French tramp doing in that bedroom?

DONOVAN: Will you shut up, Susie! I am in some pain!

SUSAN: I will not shut up!

DONOVAN: Aaagh! You're severing my head, woman!

NORA: Stand still, you brute you, or I'll hop the stick off you!

DONOVAN: Madam, I am not an animal!

NORA: You're not indeed, Doctor. I'm sorry.
(SUSAN *dashes to* TIM.)

SUSAN: I want to know what the hell's going on between you
and that woman in there! And I want to know now,
Timmy!
(*The big door suddenly bursts open—*JACK, *pretending he is the
German, and guldering.*)

JACK: I hear you sell your house, Herr Gallagher—ja? I give you
a fortune to buy it.
(*The moment the door opens, the lamp, which* TIM *is holding in*

his hand, flickers a few times and now dies. SUSAN *screams. For three seconds the stage is in total darkness. During this total blackout:)*

NORA: Will you close that big door, Barney! You've blown the lamp out!

DONOVAN: Get that foreign brute out of here!

NORA: Has anybody got a box of matches?

(*Now sneak the lights up to half. The assumption will be that the stage is still in total darkness. The actors behave as if it were.* JACK *is now inside and closes both doors behind him.* CLAIRE *has entered from the bedroom.*)

SUSAN: Daddy?!

DONOVAN: You're quite safe, darling. Just keep away from the German.

NORA: Have you got the lamp, Tim?

CLAIRE: (*Into* TIM'*s ear*) I understand perfectly.

SUSAN: (*Pointing in the wrong direction*) I hear her! She's there!

JACK: A million Deutschmark, Herr Gallagher. I hoffer you any monies you hask for.

TIM: O my God.

(*Blackout. Music.*)

ACT TWO

The action is continuous. Everybody is in the same position as at the end of Act 1. And everybody wants to establish his/her own bearings and then the bearings of everybody else.

JACK: (*Loudly*) A million Deutschmark, Herr Gallagher. I hoffer you any monies you hask for.

TIM: O my God.

SUSAN: Where are you, Daddy?

DONOVAN: Here, darling. (*Trying to turn round*) Ooogh.

TIM: (*Whispers*) Jack?

JACK: (*Loudly*) Herr Gallagher? Ja?

TIM: (*Whispers*) Stop that German stuff!

DONOVAN: Put that damned light on!

NORA: Have you got the lamp, Tim?

TIM: I think it's on the table. (*Whispers*) Jack?
    (CLAIRE *is now beside* TIM. *She nibbles his ear.*)
    Who's that? Who's that?

CLAIRE: (*Whispers*) It's unbelievable, isn't it?

TIM: Oh, hello, Susan. How are you?

CLAIRE: (*French accent*) 'ello, my big 'andsome Jack.

TIM: (*Whispers*) Claire, damn you—!
    (*She slips away from him.* NORA DAN *is groping at the table.*)

NORA: It's not here, Tim.

TIM: It must be.

SUSAN: Daddy?

DONOVAN: Over here, Susie.
    (JACK *is feeling in front of him, trying to go towards* TIM'*s voice.*)

JACK: Herr Gallagher?

TIM: (*Whispers*) Cut it out, Jack!

NORA: No, it's not here. Has anybody got a match?
   (JACK's *groping hands now find a figure*—CLAIRE's.)
JACK: Susan?
TIM: There are matches on the mantelpiece, Nora.
JACK: Susan? It's Jack. How's it all going?
CLAIRE: It's not Susan. It's Evette.
JACK: You're here? Christ!
   (*Again she slips away.*)
   When did you arrive . . .?
NORA: You get them for me, Tim.
TIM: I can't—that fire attacks me.
NORA: Attacks you? What are you blathering about?
   (JACK's *hands now find another figure*—SUSAN's.)
JACK: Hold on, Evette. When did you—?
SUSAN: Take your filthy hands off me, you hun! Daddy!
JACK: Susan, it's—
SUSAN: Daddy!
DONOVAN: Protect my daughter, Tim! Protect my only child!
   Ooogh.
   (SUSAN *finds her way to her father.* CLAIRE *slips upstairs.* TIM
   and JACK *find one another.*)
TIM: Jack?
JACK: Herr Gallagher!
TIM: Drop that accent.
NORA: Have you no matches, Barney?
TIM: (*German accent*) Sorry. No. I don't have none matches.
JACK: I'm supposed to be the German, you fool!
TIM: You're not Willie Hausenbach any more!
JACK: Who?
TIM: Barney Munich—Barney the Banks. You're an eejit.
JACK: *I'm* an eejit?!
TIM: Jack the Cod—a local fisherman—a fool—you can't fish for
   nuts.
JACK: Tim—
TIM: The German has been here! Get out, man!
JACK: Tim—
TIM: And the Doctor thinks I'm going to sell this house to him,
   or at least a site—

61

SUSAN: Please put the lights on!

TIM: —and I'm an expert scrambler and they're both coming back tomorrow for the weekend and Hausenbach's a transvestite and—

JACK: Shut up and listen to me!

NORA: Will none of yous give me a hand?

JACK: Your time is up! Get them all out!

TIM: I can't. The Doctor's anchored to the wall.

JACK: Evette's here, man!

TIM: Don't I know. Chewing my ear all evening—

JACK: Evette?

TIM: Yes, damn her. And pulling her underwear out of my pocket.

JACK: Evette?!

(NORA DAN *strikes a match.*)

NORA: Ah, that's a bit better. (*To* TIM) And you had the lamp after all.

TIM: Where?

NORA: Where, he says. Isn't it in your hand! God bless us, Tim, are you soft in the head? Take the globe off it.

DONOVAN: I have been wronged.

NORA: You have been wronged surely, Doctor. But we'll soon get you sorted.

(*The lamp is now lit.*)

That's grand. Now we know where we're at. (*Seeing* JACK) And it's you's in it, Jack? God forgive you imitating poor Barney the Banks like that.

(*She places the lamp on the table.*)

SUSAN: (*To* JACK) What are you doing here?

DONOVAN: Who is it, Susie?

TIM: It's Jack the Cod.

JACK: What's that man doing down there?

SUSAN: That's Daddy.

NORA: He was imitating a cow for us—weren't you? And he did it very well, too.

JACK: Doctor Donovan?!

NORA: The Doctor surely. He's a wee bit cross, the creature; naturally.

SUSAN: For God's sake, Jack, help him. He's chained there.

DONOVAN: It's the village blacksmith I need—not the village idiot!

NORA: (*To* JACK) A wee bit upset, the soul. But he'll come round.

JACK: (*To* TIM) Where's Evette?

TIM: Evette?

SUSAN: The French woman?

JACK: Yes.

SUSAN: You've met her?

JACK: Yes. Have you?

SUSAN: She's here! With him!

JACK: With Tim?

SUSAN: With Tim indeed—instead of in her husband's caravan. No wonder he (TIM) looks so hangdog!

JACK: Evette's husband is here, too?

SUSAN: Why wouldn't he be? He lives here!

JACK: Good God!

NORA: Will yous all keep quiet and listen to me. I've the solution to the whole thing.

DONOVAN: Ooogh.

SUSAN: Nora Dan, will you please go on your bike and get help somewhere?

NORA: That's what I'm going to do. The man with the smartest pair of hands about here is Barney the Banks—he'll have the Doctor free in no time at all. (*To* TIM) Slip you over and get him.

DONOVAN: I will not be rescued by that brute!

NORA: Indeed and you will, Doctor, and glad to be, too. (*To* TIM) Away you go on the bike. The caravan's just across the banks.

SUSAN: (*To* TIM) Will you please hurry!

TIM: I hardly know him. I couldn't ask him.

NORA: You couldn't ask him. Well, I'll ask him then. Come on. Give me a lift over.

TIM: Me?!

JACK: Off you go, expert scrambler.

SUSAN: Will you go, Timmy!

NORA: He thinks I'm nervous, the creature.

63

TIM: You're terrified!

NORA: You don't know Nora Dan, son.

TIM: I've no licence.

NORA: He has no licence.

> (*She takes his arm and leads him to the door.*)
> Sure nobody about here has either licence or insurance.
> (*To* JACK) Mind the lamp when I open the door. The
> draught in this aul byre would clean corn. Come on, Tim.
> Barney'll be glad to help.

TIM: Jack, please—

SUSAN: Will you hurry, Timmy!

NORA: We'll be back in five minutes.

TIM: If we're not, you'll know—

SUSAN: Go on, Timmy! Move!

> (NORA *leads* TIM *outside and closes both doors behind her.*
> SUSAN *sits dejectedly on a stool.* JACK *puts the lamp back on the
> table. Sound of the motorbike starting up, cutting out, starting
> up again. Furious revving—the engine stutters—more revving.
> The bike moves off erratically.*)

DONOVAN: Ooogh.

JACK: Nora Dan should be wearing a helmet.

SUSAN: And Timmy.

JACK: Well . . .

> (JACK *now moves around the kitchen. His concern is: where is*
> EVETTE?)

DONOVAN: I'm getting very cold. Are there any spirits in the
house?

JACK: (*To* SUSAN) There's vodka there somewhere.

> (*He peers into the bedroom and whispers,* Evette?
> SUSAN *pours a drink and brings it to* DONOVAN.)

DONOVAN: What's that?

SUSAN: Vodka.

DONOVAN: I hate vodka.

SUSAN: That's all there is.

DONOVAN: Have they far to go?

SUSAN: I don't know.

DONOVAN: Where's this caravan?

SUSAN: I don't know.

DONOVAN: You're such a consolation, Susie. Could you at least manage to keep the fire going?—ooogh.

(*She returns to her stool.*)

SUSAN: I think I'm going to cry, Jack.

JACK: No, you're not.

SUSAN: And everything was going so perfectly. Daddy just loved the place—thought it was unbelievable.

(JACK *peers up the well of the stairs.*)

JACK: (*Whispers*) Evette?

SUSAN: I was even planning to come back this way tomorrow and spend the weekend here. Timmy was all for it; thought it was a great idea. Do you think he meant it, Jack?

JACK: Of course.

SUSAN: Why would he say it if he didn't mean it? I just don't know any more. He sounded as if he meant it. He even promised he'd take me scrambling on Nora Dan's bike.

JACK: My bike, you mean.

SUSAN: No, Nora Dan's.

JACK: Nora Dan has no bike, for God's sake. That's my bike. He told you it was his? The fool can't even drive!

SUSAN: But he's away driving on it now . . .

(*Concern*) My God, he'll have an accident, Jack!

JACK: (*Peering into settle bed; whispers*) Evette?

SUSAN: (*Anger*) My God, I hope he does! Oh, the liar! And of course, of course she's not Nora the Scrambler! How did I believe that?!—ex-champion of Donegal! O my God! Is there running water in this house?

JACK: No.

SUSAN: Another lie! And I'm sure you have a smoothing iron, haven't you?

JACK: Yes.

SUSAN: More lies! My God, I hate him! And d'you know what he told me, too?—he does her washing!

JACK: Nora Dan's?

SUSAN: That woman he has living with him here—that French tramp! Lies, lies, lies—that's all he has told me since I got here!

DONOVAN: Susie?

SUSAN: I'm putting turf on the fire, Daddy. (*To* JACK) Why didn't you tell me he was such a skilled liar, Jack? (JACK *now goes to her.*)

JACK: She was here in the house when you arrived?

SUSAN: Walking around as if she owned the place; chatting and laughing with Daddy; flirting openly with Timmy. He wants to humiliate me, Jack!

JACK: Describe her.

SUSAN: She's common looking, vulgar, brazen manner—

JACK: About 28, 29?

SUSAN: Yes.

JACK: Average height?

SUSAN: Yes.

JACK: Blonde?

SUSAN: It's not natural.

JACK: Round-faced?

SUSAN: Do you know her?

JACK: Absolutely.

SUSAN: She has hardly any English.

JACK: She was born and bred in Omagh.

SUSAN: Her name is Evette.

JACK: Her name is Claire Harkin.

SUSAN: She's married to a German.

JACK: She's single. She's in the English Department with Master Timothy.

SUSAN: But I met her husband!

JACK: In fact she's an old girlfriend of Master Timothy's from years back.

SUSAN: So all that stuff about . . .? And everything he said about . . .? And that German character isn't her husband at . . .? Oh, the bastard! The rotten, lying bastard! (*Cries.*) There! I told you I was going to cry!

JACK: Shhh.

SUSAN: I hope he never gets his bloody thesis finished! I hope they kick him out of that miserable bloody job! I hope he comes off that bike and breaks his bloody neck!

JACK: (*His arms around her*) Shhh.

SUSAN: God, how I loathe him!

JACK: I know—I know.

SUSAN: I don't really mean that at all, Jack—I mean about his thesis and his miserable job.

JACK: Of course you don't.

SUSAN: But I mean all the rest.

JACK: I know—shhh—I know—I know. (*A quick furtive look at his watch.*) This has been a very unfortunate experience, Susan. You have been treated shabbily. But the important thing now is to protect you from further hurt.

DONOVAN: Ooogh.

JACK: (*Offering handkerchief*) Here.

SUSAN: Thanks.

JACK: May I tell you something?

SUSAN: What?

JACK: Many, many years ago, Susan, you and I were fortunate enough to experience and share an affection that is still one of my most sustaining memories. And when we broke up— and I can tell you this now; indeed I embrace the opportunity to make this declaration, however unhappy, however unlikely the circumstances for this kind of confession—but when we broke up—and I suspect that you would be the first to admit that I wasn't exclusively to blame for that unfortunate episode—but when it happened —and I say this now very deliberately and with absolute sincerity—when it happened, Susan, a part of me died.

SUSAN: Oh, Jack. (*Sobs.*) I'm off again.

JACK: Does that sound maudlin?

SUSAN: No.

JACK: Is this the wrong time to say it?

SUSAN: I thought it all meant nothing to you.

JACK: We could have been quite a pair.

SUSAN: Could we?

JACK: We're alike in so many ways.

SUSAN: Are we?

JACK: So alike it's . . . uncanny. Susan, will you trust me?

DONOVAN: Ooogh.

SUSAN: Poor Daddy's in agony.

JACK: Will you trust me, Susan?

SUSAN: Yes.

JACK: You must leave here immediately.

SUSAN: But Daddy's—!

JACK: I'll release him. But you must both leave the minute he's free. What I'm really talking about, Susan, is your safety. You must be protected from Tim.

SUSAN: My safety?

JACK: That's what brought me here today—to warn you.

DONOVAN: What's keeping them, Susie?

SUSAN: They'll be back soon. (*To* JACK) Warn me?

JACK: He's had a breakdown.

SUSAN: Timmy? When?

JACK: Acute hallucinatory trauma. Cracked up suddenly last Saturday night. We were at a party. Went crazy. Tried to demolish the house—literally. It's a combination of several factors: drinking too much; pressure of work; that damned thesis he's never going to finish. Those lies you talk about—they're not lies to him—he believes them. The psychiatrist says he must have six months' total rest.

SUSAN: Oh, poor Timmy.

JACK: Poor Timmy indeed. But the important thing is: you must be gone before he returns. Right?

SUSAN: Yes.

JACK: (*Rising*) They'll soon be back. Bring that lamp over, will you?

(*He stoops down and puts his hands on her face.*)

Trust me, Susan, will you?

SUSAN: Absolutely.

(*He kisses her forehead.*)

JACK: Thank you, Susan.

(*He goes to* DONOVAN. *She follows with the lamp.*)

Well, Doctor. You got yourself tied up somehow, did you?

DONOVAN: Do you really think so?

JACK: Let's see can we help you.

DONOVAN: Are you a blacksmith?

JACK: Not quite. But we'll soon have you freed. Let's have a look. This is the trouble, is it?

SUSAN: It's that clasp. It won't open.

DONOVAN: Who is this?

SUSAN: It's Jack, Daddy.

DONOVAN: Jack the Cod—wonderful! The village idiot—why not!

SUSAN: Jack McNeilis, Daddy. You remember Jack, don't you?

JACK: How are you, Doctor?

DONOVAN: What's he doing here?

SUSAN: He's trying to help you.

DONOVAN: What's keeping Tim and that female cattle-drover?

SUSAN: She said they'd be back in five minutes.

DONOVAN: They've gone at least an hour. The circulation isn't reaching the feet. I've lost all feeling in the feet and legs.

JACK: Yes—it's that hook. If I could prize it open— (*To* SUSAN) There's a pair of pliers in the drawer of the dresser.

DONOVAN: Careful!

JACK: Sorry—sorry. These chains haven't been used for over sixty years, not since my father was a boy.

DONOVAN: What was your father doing here?

JACK: He lived here until he was seven. (*To* SUSAN) Thanks.

DONOVAN: So Tim bought it from your father?

JACK: I'm afraid Tim has been telling you all a lot of fibs, Doctor. I've just been explaining to Susan: Tim's a very sick man.

SUSAN: He's had a breakdown.

DONOVAN: God.

JACK: This is my house. I let Tim have it for the weekend.

DONOVAN: Do you hear this, Susie?

SUSAN: Jack's just told me. It's terrible. Apparently he can get very violent.

DONOVAN: Good God. The bloody German wasn't so slow.

JACK: He spotted it?

DONOVAN: He certainly did.

JACK: I suppose a stranger would see the symptoms more clearly. Anyhow, the important thing now is to get you freed. Could you move your head just slightly . . .? That's it! That's better! Now if I can prize this open. . . . (*As he works*) Wonderful place this, isn't it, Doctor? You're an antiquarian yourself, aren't you?

DONOVAN: Careful . . .

JACK: You're all right. Just sit still . . .
  (CLAIRE *comes downstairs, goes to the clothes-line and hangs up tights. She then goes into the bedroom.*)
  Yes, this is where we all come from, isn't it? This is our first cathedral. This shaped all our souls.
DONOVAN: This determined our first priorities! This is our native simplicity! Don't give me that shit!
SUSAN: Daddy!
DONOVAN: Forgive me, Susie. (*To* JACK) Stop mouthing, you fool. This is the greatest dump in all—Aaagh! My neck! My neck!
JACK: Sorry. You—
DONOVAN: You've pierced my neck!
JACK: I'm sorry, Doctor, but you moved your—
DONOVAN: Look at the blood! Get him away from me!
SUSAN: (*To* JACK) Maybe we'd better—
DONOVAN: Keep that fool away from me, Susie!
SUSAN: We'll wait for the others, Jack.
DONOVAN: Get me something to bind the wound!
  (SUSAN *dashes into the centre of the kitchen, looks around in panic, sees the tights on the line, grabs them and returns to* DONOVAN.)
  O God, dear God, let me survive this night.
JACK: (*To* DONOVAN) I'm sorry, Doctor. It was an accident.
DONOVAN: Leave me. Leave me.
SUSAN: There you are, Daddy. That's all I can find.
DONOVAN: (*As he wraps the tights around his neck*) Thank you. Now please leave me.
  (SUSAN *takes* JACK's *arm and leads him away.*)
JACK: He moved his bloody head just as I was—
SUSAN: I know—I know. He's better left alone.
DONOVAN: (*Sings*) Abide with me! Fast falls the eventide;
             The darkness deepens: Lord, with me abide!
             When other helpers fail, and comforts flee,
             Help of the helpless, O abide with me!
  (*After the first line of the hymn:*)
JACK: God, what a day!
SUSAN: What's keeping the others? Didn't Nora Dan say they'd—

(*She suddenly breaks off—she hears* CLAIRE *singing the hymn with* THE DOCTOR.)

SUSAN: Listen!

JACK: What?

SUSAN: There she is! Evette—Claire—she's in there!

JACK: Where?

SUSAN: In that room there!

(JACK *dashes to the bedroom door.*)

JACK: Come out at once, Claire. I know you're in there. (*To* SUSAN) Give me that lamp. (*To* CLAIRE) This nonsense has got to end now.

(SUSAN *is crossing with the lamp when the big door bursts open. The lamp flickers and dies.* DONOVAN *stops singing.*)

Damnit—that bloody latch!

SUSAN: Jaaaack . . .?

JACK: You're perfectly all right, Susan. Just stand where you are. Don't move.

DONOVAN: Put that light on!

SUSAN: Please, Jack . . .

DONOVAN: What are you doing, McNeilis?

SUSAN: Daddy?

DONOVAN: Susie, come over here, darling—ooogh . . .

JACK: Keep calm, Susan. Everything's in hand.

SUSAN: I'm frightened, Jack.

DONOVAN: I'm warning you, McNeilis—lay one finger on that child and—

JACK: I'm looking for the lamp, Doctor. Where are you, Susan?

(EVETTE *enters. She is a sophisticated, stylish woman in her early thirties. She is carrying a small weekend case. She is French but her English is perfect.*)

SUSAN: Here. I'm here.

JACK: Where? Keep talking.

SUSAN: Hello.

EVETTE: Hello.

JACK: Hello–hello.

EVETTE: Hello, Jack.

JACK: Good. Again—again.

EVETTE: Hello–hello–hello—is that enough?

71

SUSAN: Who's that?

JACK: Have you any matches?

EVETTE: I have a lighter.

JACK: Good.

SUSAN: It's her! (*Pointing in the wrong direction.*) There she is! Catch her!

(JACK *reaches out and grabs the figure beside him*—EVETTE.)

JACK: Now, Claire.

EVETTE: What are you doing in the dark?

JACK: We've had enough of your vicious little pranks.

EVETTE: There's the lighter. Aren't you glad to see me?

SUSAN: Jack, I don't think it's—

JACK: It's quite all right, Susan. Just bring the lamp over here.

EVETTE: Susan? Who's Susan?

JACK: I warned you you were going to ruin Tim's career. But I'm made of sterner stuff, Claire.

(*He lights the lighter. And at that moment* CLAIRE *is crossing towards the stairs.*)

EVETTE: Claire? Who's Claire?

SUSAN: There she is, Jack! (*Now seeing* EVETTE.) But who's she?

(JACK *has now lit the lamp.*)

JACK: Now, Miss Harkin.

SUSAN: Where did she come from?

JACK: Christ.

EVETTE: You said you'd meet me at the bus.

SUSAN: Who's she, Jack?

DONOVAN: Ooogh.

EVETTE: What's that?!

CLAIRE: (*Ascending the stairs; sings*) 'Abide with me! Fast falls the eventide . . .'

DONOVAN: Who's that?

CLAIRE: (*To* DONOVAN) Evette. (*She continues singing.*)

SUSAN: That's her! There she is!

EVETTE: Who's that?

JACK: That's Claire.

SUSAN: Who are you?

JACK: That's Evette.

EVETTE: Who is she?

72

JACK: That's Susan.

EVETTE: You didn't tell me you were going to have a party, Jack!

DONOVAN: Ooogh.

EVETTE: Who's that?

JACK: That's Susan's father.

EVETTE: What's he doing down there?

JACK: I think he's imitating a cow.

EVETTE: You're playing charades!

JACK: No. He's chained himself there.

EVETTE: Why?

JACK: How would I know! Because—don't ask me—because he thought this was a cathedral.

DONOVAN: This is an evil house.

EVETTE: That's Teddy's voice!

SUSAN: Whose?

EVETTE: What's Teddy doing here?

JACK: Who's Teddy?

DONOVAN: Is that the female cattle-drover?

EVETTE: Yes! It is Teddy!

(*She runs to* DONOVAN *and crouches down beside him.*)

It's me, Teddy. It's Evette.

DONOVAN: Ooogh.

EVETTE: What's the matter with you?

SUSAN: (*To* JACK) Do you know her?

JACK: Yes.

SUSAN: Is she drunk?

JACK: Don't think so.

EVETTE: Look at me, Teddy.

DONOVAN: Who is it?

EVETTE: Evette! Evette! Why are you hiding down here?

DONOVAN: A third phrase, Evette. Very good. Excellent.

EVETTE: A third phrase? What do you mean? (*To the others*) Is he drunk?

DONOVAN: Not that language matters when you're as young and as beautiful as you are.

EVETTE: What language, Teddy? What are you talking about? And why have you those tights around your neck? (*To* JACK) What's going on here, Jack?

73

DONOVAN: Words are superfluous.

EVETTE: (*To* DONOVAN) What words? (*To the others*) Is he delirious? (*Very slowly and distinctly to* DONOVAN) It's Evette, Teddy. Evette Giroux. We went to Brussels together last month for my birthday—remember? Look—this is the watch you bought me there.

DONOVAN: (*Realizing*) Ooogh.

SUSAN: Who is this woman?

JACK: Shhh.

SUSAN: Did you ask her here?

JACK: Me? Never! Shhh.

EVETTE: You remember this watch, don't you?

DONOVAN: Who is this woman?

EVETTE: Look—you had it inscribed at the back.

DONOVAN: Take this woman away. She is a little bit gallagher.

EVETTE: Teddy, I'm—

DONOVAN: Take her away and talk to her soft.

EVETTE: He *is* delirious. (*She dashes to* JACK *and* SUSAN.) He doesn't know me! Look—(*the watch*)—the inscription and the date. We're old friends. We've known each other for ages and ages. He's taking me to Washington with him next Friday!

SUSAN: Daddy?

EVETTE: He's your—? Then you're his daughter, Susan! He told me all about you. You're going with a wastrel called Timmy.

SUSAN: His name isn't Teddy. It's Patrick Mary Pious.

EVETTE: I know—I know—Teddy's my pet name for him—short for Teddybear. But he told me you and he were going to Sligo this weekend?

SUSAN: It's unbelievable, Jack.

JACK: Have you the audacity, indeed may I say the insolence, to ask Susan and myself to subscribe to the patently absurd proposition that you and Senator Donovan have, over a considerable period of time—

DONOVAN: Ooogh.

SUSAN: You mean to say that last month you and Daddy were in Brussels together and next Friday you're going to—?

74

DONOVAN: Ooogh.

SUSAN: Jack, I'm going to cry.

JACK: No, you're not.

EVETTE: Why didn't you tell me Teddy was going to be here?

JACK: He wasn't to be here.

EVETTE: And who's that woman up there?

JACK: That's Tim's girlfriend.

EVETTE: She's Tim's girlfriend!

SUSAN: I certainly am not!

EVETTE: How many more women have you got here?

JACK: How dare you speak to me like that!

SUSAN: She's shameless—she followed him here.

EVETTE: I was invited here—by him (JACK).

JACK: That's a lie.

SUSAN: Is she your girlfriend?

JACK: She certainly is not!

DONOVAN: Ooogh.

EVETTE: How can you stand about talking? Poor Teddy's ill!

    (CLAIRE *comes downstairs.*)

SUSAN: There she is, Jack! Look—there she is! O dear God—
    (*Begins sobbing.*) There. I told you I was going to cry.
    (*Both doors suddenly burst open.*)

CLAIRE: Watch the lamp!

JACK: Watch the lamp! Claire, come here, Claire!

    (TIM, BARNEY *and* NORA DAN *enter noisily.* NORA DAN *is*
    between TIM *and* BARNEY, *her arms around their shoulders.*
    She has one foot raised off the ground. TIM, *too, is dishevelled*
    from the tumble off the bike. BARNEY *is very excited and*
    because of his excitement he behaves as if he were at a party:
    shouting, laughing, etc.

    As they enter everybody talks simultaneously.)

BARNEY: We have a little accident here, ha–ha–ha.

CLAIRE: Nora!

NORA: Slow, now, slow, slow.

CLAIRE: What happened, Nora?

TIM: I crashed into the caravan.

CLAIRE: Is she hurt?

NORA: I want to see the doctor.

EVETTE: Who are these people, Jack?

CLAIRE: Are you hurt, Nora?

(NORA *is brought to the settle bed and laid down there.*)

NORA: I'm not too bad.

DONOVAN: Ooogh.

NORA: Ooogh.

DONOVAN: Go ahead! Ridicule me!

NORA: Is that you, Doctor?

SUSAN: (*Sobbing*) It's unbelievable—unbelievable.

CLAIRE: (*To* SUSAN) Stop that at once!

SUSAN: (*Louder*) Ooogh.

NORA: I'll be all right when I lie down.

BARNEY: I am sitting very private with my book and suddenly—boom!

JACK: Tie those curtains back.

TIM: (*To* JACK) I got it started all right but I couldn't stop it.

BARNEY: I think my caravan is bombed—ha–ha–ha!

CLAIRE: (*To* JACK) Is there any spirits in the house?

JACK: I've some whiskey in my bag.

(*He goes off to the bedroom.* CLAIRE *takes control.*)

NORA: I'm afraid we damaged poor Barney's caravan.

BARNEY: No, no; it does not matter.

CLAIRE: Just ease yourself back there, Nora. You're fine.

NORA: I'm fine surely, thanks be to God.

CLAIRE: Where are you hurt?

NORA: It's the leg. It must be broken.

DONOVAN: What's happening back there?

SUSAN: (*To* DONOVAN) They came off the motorbike. Nora Dan has broken her leg.

DONOVAN: Damn her leg. Did they bring a blacksmith?

BARNEY: (*To* EVETTE) Hello. My name is Willie. In English that is Barney.

EVETTE: Evette.

BARNEY: Evette? Good, ha–ha–ha. (*Pointing to* CLAIRE) Evette also. (*Pointing to* SUSAN) Also Evette. Perhaps is every Irish girl named Evette?

CLAIRE: (*To* TIM) Are you all right?

TIM: I think so.

CLAIRE: There's a hot-water bottle upstairs.

TIM: Where?

CLAIRE: At the foot of the bed.

(*He goes upstairs.*)

BARNEY: (*To* EVETTE) Welcome to handsome Ballybeg. (*The gesture.*)

CLAIRE: We'll have the Doctor with you in a second, Nora. (*To* BARNEY) See can you release the Doctor, Barney.

BARNEY: Release the Doctor?

CLAIRE: There he is.

(BARNEY *now sees* THE DOCTOR *for the first time.*)

BARNEY: Ah! I see him!

EVETTE: He's chained.

BARNEY: Good. He was naughty, ja? Ha–ha–ha.

(JACK *returns to* CLAIRE *with the whiskey.*)

JACK: Here you are.

CLAIRE: Thanks. Get me a cup.

(TIM *returns with the hot-water bottle.*)

TIM: (*To* JACK, *with great enthusiasm*) That's a terrific bike. I'm going to save up for one.

CLAIRE: Now, Nora.

JACK: Is it damaged?

TIM: I don't think so— (*Sees* EVETTE.) Who's that?

JACK: Evette. Tim Gallagher.

TIM: Ah. You're the real French tramp.

EVETTE: And you're Tim the wastrel.

TIM: You're welcome.

CLAIRE: (*To* TIM) Did you get it?

TIM: Coming. Here it is.

CLAIRE: For God's sake it's no good empty. Fill it.

(*He goes to the fireplace. The usual consequences:* O my God, *etc. while this is happening:*)

BARNEY: So we encounter again, Doctor?

DONOVAN: Who is this?

SUSAN: It's Barney the Banks. He's going to—

DONOVAN: Get him away from me! Don't touch me, you—

SUSAN: Daddy, stop it! Stop it at once!

DONOVAN: I will not be—

77

SUSAN: (*To* BARNEY) Don't listen to him. It's that clasp. It won't open.
BARNEY: You punish him because he is bold? Ha–ha–ha. (*To* DONOVAN) Bold doctor—ja?
DONOVAN: Ooogh.
CLAIRE: How do you feel now, Nora?
NORA: I'm coming round slowly. Is the room very cold?
CLAIRE: It's the shock. Hurry up, Tim.
NORA: It's the shock surely. Do you think the ankle's broken?
CLAIRE: You probably just twisted it. We'll get the doctor to look at it.
TIM: (*Coughing*) There.
CLAIRE: Are you sure you're all right?
TIM: Yes.
CLAIRE: Now, Nora. That'll warm you up.
NORA: Thank you, Tim.
CLAIRE: That's better, isn't it?
NORA: I don't think I'll ever rise from this bed again.
CLAIRE: Indeed you will. Here—a spoonful of whiskey.
NORA: A spoonful of whiskey surely. Yous have me spoiled. O dear, O dear, O dear, I doubt if I'll ever be fit to leave this house again.
BARNEY: (*To* DONOVAN) I have it now nearly. One more minute.
JACK: What did she say there? Did that old bitch just say she'd never—
CLAIRE: For God's sake can't you lower your voice?
JACK: (*Whispering*) I will not lower my voice in my own house! I know what she's up to. She thinks she's going to squat here. Well it's not going to work!
CLAIRE: Jack, she's hurt.
JACK: I don't give a damn if she's paralysed! She gets out of here in five minutes!
CLAIRE: I'm Claire. You're Evette.
EVETTE: How do you know that?
CLAIRE: I understand perfectly.
EVETTE: You're Tim's girlfriend, aren't you?
CLAIRE: Am I?
JACK: You all get out of here in five minutes!
EVETTE: Me, too?

JACK: Especially you.

EVETTE: Happily.

JACK: You and everybody.

BARNEY: There we are! Dr Bollocks is liberated!

SUSAN: (*To* BARNEY) Thank you very much.

BARNEY: My pleasure, Evette—ha–ha–ha.

SUSAN: (*To* DONOVAN) Can you stand? Give me your arm.

EVETTE: Lean on me, Teddy.

DONOVAN: Ooogh.

> (*He gets slowly to his feet. From now on he holds his head to the side. The legs of the tights dangle down his back.*)

SUSAN: You're all right, aren't you?

DONOVAN: I think so.

SUSAN: It was Barney that got you free.

DONOVAN: I'll survive. (*To* BARNEY) Thank you.

BARNEY: Do not be bold again, Doctor—ja? Ha–ha–ha.

DONOVAN: (*To* SUSAN) Get the cases.

CLAIRE: Would you take a look at Nora, Doctor?

DONOVAN: I'm in a hurry.

CLAIRE: She has hurt her leg.

DONOVAN: Where is she?

CLAIRE: Over here.

DONOVAN: What happened to her?

SUSAN: She came off her bike—Timmy's bike—Jack's bike.

DONOVAN: Wouldn't one tumble have sufficed?

> (TIM *takes the tights from* DONOVAN's *neck.*)

TIM: I don't think you need these any . . .

> (*He holds them in his hands. Everybody looks at him. Pause. Then he stuffs them into his pocket.*)

They dried. On your neck.

DONOVAN: Not only are you deranged. You are despicable.

BARNEY: May I have a little vodka to celebrate that Nora Dan fall?

JACK: Why not. Help yourself. Make yourself at home.

BARNEY: Thank you. Thank you.

JACK: Anybody else for a drink? Whiskey? Vodka? It's open house!

NORA: It's my ankle, Doctor. It's throbbing and it's hot.

DONOVAN: Are you in pain?

NORA: Pain surely, Doctor. I must have come down heavy on it.

DONOVAN: Can you move it?

NORA: Not a budge, Doctor.

DONOVAN: (*Moving it vigorously*) Indeed you can.

NORA: Lord, Doctor, that's terrible sore. Is it broken?

DONOVAN: Not at all. A slight sprain. Rest it over the weekend. (*Moving away from the bed.*) My case is somewhere . . .

CLAIRE: Are you sure she's all right?

DONOVAN: Your English is suddenly very fluent.

CLAIRE: Are you certain nothing's broken?

DONOVAN: My neck is.

(*He exits to the bedroom.*)

EVETTE: Let me help you, Teddy? (*Exits.*)

JACK: Open house. Wander around. Come and go as you wish.

SUSAN: When are you going home?

JACK: Tonight—now—if my bike's working.

SUSAN: Will you take me with you?

JACK: Absolutely. But what about—

SUSAN: I'm not going with him if she's going with him!

BARNEY: (*To* TIM) You are feeling not so frisky now, Herr McNeilis?

TIM: Yes—no—I'm fine, thanks.

BARNEY: So perhaps maybe tomorrow I come and talk to you about selling this house from you?

JACK: Why not! Just give it to him for Christ's sake!

BARNEY: No, no, I buy it—I buy it correct. Ja? (*Catching the legs of the tights*) 'To us lovers everywhere'—ha–ha–ha.

(DONOVAN *and* EVETTE *enter.*)

DONOVAN: Are you ready, Susie?

SUSAN: Is she going with you?

EVETTE: I'm not staying here!

SUSAN: Then I'll go home with Jack.

DONOVAN: You'll come with me.

JACK: I'll be happy to drive her home, Doctor—that is, of course, with your permission.

(DONOVAN *surveys them all slowly. Pause. Then:*)

DONOVAN: Never in all my life . . . in my long career as a

politician and a doctor I have never—

NORA: Doctor!

DONOVAN: (*To* BARNEY) I am grateful to you for rescuing me, sir. But I must also say that this island has no need at all for land-grabbing transvestites of your calibre.

BARNEY: Thank you, Doctor. Ha–ha–ha.

DONOVAN: I have no idea what your wife's (CLAIRE) game is—

BARNEY: Evette? Ja–ja.

DONOVAN: Whatever alias she uses. She is clearly a liar and a schemer and I think you are well matched.

TIM: (*Whispers to* JACK) What's he talking about? Is he cracking up?

NORA: Doctor!

DONOVAN: (*To* TIM) As for you; I accept that you are a very ill man. But I must say this to you: if you ever darken my door again, I will have you arrested.

NORA: Doctor!

EVETTE: The lady in the bed wants you.

DONOVAN: Well?

NORA: Could I have a word with you, Doctor?

DONOVAN: I've told you: you're perfectly well but much too old for scrambling.

NORA: Could the rest of yous move away . . .?

(DONOVAN *and* NORA *are now alone together.*)

DONOVAN: What is it? What is it?

NORA: I was just thinking, Doctor, now that I'm going to be an invalid here, I'll not be needing my own house.

DONOVAN: Well?

NORA: It's just across the fields there. Two rooms and an acre of land overlooking the strand. The very place you're looking for, Doctor!

DONOVAN: Oh Jesus Christ—let me out of . . .!

(*He grabs his case and almost runs out of the house.*)

EVETTE: Hold on, Teddy! I'm coming! I'm coming!

(*She follows him.*)

CLAIRE: Watch the lamp!

JACK: Watch the lamp!

(JACK *closes both doors after them.*)

TIM: (*Worried*) What does he mean—I'm a very ill man. I only got a scratch on my head.

CLAIRE: You've missed the last bus.

TIM: (*Looking at his watch*) My watch has stopped. What time is it?

CLAIRE: It's gone.

TIM: I'll just have to stay then.

CLAIRE: Yes.

TIM: The whole weekend. After all.

CLAIRE: Yes.

TIM: Is there room?

CLAIRE: When they leave, there is.

TIM: I'd better ask Jack.

(*She begins to make tea.*)

BARNEY: I must depart also. My caravan has a big bump to hammer out. You feel not too bad now, Nora?

NORA: Not too bad surely, Barney.

BARNEY: Good. I come to see you in the morning. (*To* JACK) Thank you for the vodka. I leave this (*cup*) on the gulder. Goodnight, Evette—and Evette—ha–ha–ha. Goodnight, Herr McNeilis (TIM) and your house guest (JACK). (*To* TIM) I come to talk with you tomorrow. (*To* JACK) And you must visit handsome Ballybeg soon again—ja?

JACK: That's very kind of you.

BARNEY: You are welcome. (*The gesture.*) (*To all*) Good night— good night. Auf Wiedersehen.

(*As he exits:*)

CLAIRE: Mind the lamp!

NORA: A grand man that, Barney; a great neighbour to all of us about here.

JACK: How's the ankle?

NORA: Fair to middling. The Doctor says I'm to put no weight on it for a week at least.

JACK: Nora, what he said was—

NORA: So would it be all right with you if I just lay here until I get my strength back?

JACK: Elizabeth's arriving tomorrow.

NORA: Isn't that providential! Sure wee Elizabeth and me get on

powerful well together. And I'll have Claire till Wednesday
—for all the attention I'll need—just a cup of tea now and
again to keep me going. Sure between yous all yous'll have
me spoiled.

JACK: Nora—

NORA: I'll take another sup of that whiskey now and maybe I'd
sleep for a while.

CLAIRE: Will I pull the curtains?

NORA: Pull the curtains surely. And good night to yous all.

CLAIRE: Sleep well, Nora.

JACK: Bitch!

SUSAN: (*To* JACK) Are you ready? I want away from this place.

JACK: All right. (*To* TIM) Where's the bike?

TIM: It's lying at the back of the caravan.

JACK: Are you sure it's not damaged?

NORA: (*From behind curtains*) Sure if it is, Barney's the man'll fix
it for you.

TIM: Susan, I—

SUSAN: (*Ignoring him*) Will you be able to take my case?

JACK: We'll manage.

SUSAN: I'll go and change.

JACK: You'll need a candle up there.

SUSAN: I'm all right.

CLAIRE: Anybody want tea?

JACK: I need a drink.

CLAIRE: Tim?

TIM: Please.

> (SUSAN *is about to take her case upstairs.*)
> Let me carry that for you.
> (*Again she ignores him. She rushes upstairs.* JACK *pours
> himself a drink and drifts over to the posts and chains.*)

JACK: What a bloody day! A total disaster in every respect. You
were right, professor—it was stupid and dangerous. But I
had one second of absolute pleasure: just after I had come
in the door and someone had lit the lamp—and there was
Dr Bollocks on his hands and knees, lamenting like a stuck
pig! That almost compensated for everything. My God, if
we'd got a picture of that! 'Senator Donovan Worships the

83

Ancestral Pieties'! Stupid bloody bastard!

(CLAIRE *hands* TIM *a cup of tea.*)

TIM: Thanks.

CLAIRE: Biscuit?

TIM: No, thanks. Amn't I all right?

CLAIRE: What do you mean?

TIM: Just that the Doctor said . . . maybe he noticed something about me. When I came off the bike I think I landed on my head.

CLAIRE: You're as right as you ever were.

(*He puts the cup down and catches her hand.*)

JACK: (*Looking at the chain*) There's nothing wrong with that clasp. What's he mouthing about? That clasp's working perfectly.

(TIM *now takes* CLAIRE'*s other hand in his.*)

CLAIRE: Are you staying?

TIM: Yes. Are you glad?

JACK: I suppose he was showing you how cows used to be chained?

CLAIRE: Yes. A very large quantity of glad.

JACK: As if he would know.

TIM: Did I say that?

JACK: Absolutely.

CLAIRE: Yes.

TIM: God. A response cry.

JACK: 'You see, what you do is this. You put the chain round the cow's neck—like this—and fasten it with this clasp here. Right?'

CLAIRE: It's been a long time, Tim.

TIM: Seven and a half years. The very week I began working on the thesis.

CLAIRE: Tim the Thesis.

JACK: Pompous bloody idiot.

CLAIRE: It's on conversation, isn't it?

TIM: Language as a ritualized act between two people.

CLAIRE: Yes.

TIM: The exchange of units of communication through an agreed code.

CLAIRE: Yes.

TIM: Fundamental to any meaningful exchange between individuals.

CLAIRE: Is it?

TIM: That's the theory.

JACK: (*Tentatively*) Tim . . .?

CLAIRE: Chat, really.

TIM: Yes.

CLAIRE: What we're doing now.

TIM: But I think that after this I may have to rewrite a lot of it.

CLAIRE: Why?

TIM: All that stuff about units of communication. Maybe the units don't matter all that much.

CLAIRE: I think that's true.

JACK: Can you come here for a minute, Tim?

TIM: We're conversing now but we're not exchanging units, are we?

CLAIRE: I don't think so, are we?

TIM: I don't think we can be because I'm not too sure what I'm saying.

CLAIRE: I don't know what you're saying either but I think I know what's implicit in it.

JACK: Tim, I think I'm in a bit of trouble.

TIM: Even if what I'm saying is rubbish?

CLAIRE: Yes.

TIM: Like 'this is our first cathedral'?

CLAIRE: Like that.

TIM: Like 'this is the true centre'?

CLAIRE: I think I know what's implicit in that.

TIM: Maybe the message doesn't matter at all then.

JACK: Tim!

CLAIRE: It's the occasion that matters.

TIM: And the reverberations that the occasion generates.

(*They have now drifted across the stage together and end up leaning very gently against the upright supporting the loft.*)

CLAIRE: I feel the reverberations.

TIM: I feel the reverberations.

CLAIRE: And the desire to sustain the occasion.

TIM: And saying anything, anything at all, that keeps the occasion going.

JACK: Tim!

CLAIRE: Maybe even saying nothing.

TIM: Maybe. Maybe silence is the perfect discourse.

CLAIRE: Kiss me then.

TIM: I can scarcely hear you. Will you kiss me, Claire?
(They kiss and hold that kiss until the play ends. As they kiss they lean heavily against the upright.)

JACK: I'm stuck, Tim! Will you for God's sake come here and—
(The upright begins to move. Sounds of timbers creaking.)
Get away from the upright, Tim! You'll bring the roof down!

SUSAN: *(Off)* Jack?

JACK: D'you hear me, Gallagher?! Get away from the upright! Susan!
(SUSAN, now dressed as in her first appearance, appears at the top of the stairs.)

SUSAN: What's happening, Jack?! The floor's shaking!
(She staggers down the shaking stairs.)

JACK: The upright, Tim! Get away from it!
(The curtains are pulled back. NORA's head appears.)

NORA: Jesus, Mary and Joseph, what's the noise?!

SUSAN: Jack!
(The big door blows open. The lamp flickers—almost dies—survives—almost dies. The sound of cracking timbers increases.)

JACK: Watch the lamp!

SUSAN: Jack, where are you, Jack?!

NORA: What's happening?

JACK: Help! I'm trapped!

NORA: Jesus, Mary and Joseph, the house is falling in!

SUSAN: Jack, the place is . . . ooogh!

JACK: O my God.
(The lamp dies. Total darkness.)